"I want to find out what that dress is hiding," Jackson whispered

Alexis smoothed her fingers down the front of his shirt, a sassy, impudent light brightening her eyes. "If you're lucky, I'll let you," she teased.

Jackson tightened his grip on her hips. With gradual pressure, he drew her closer so their bodies brushed enticingly, just enough to tantalize. "Just so you know right up front, I want to do things *with* you and *to* you that might shock you."

"I want to be shocked," she said, moving her thighs restlessly against his.

He nearly groaned as a hot jolt of awareness settled low. "You'll do whatever I want?" he continued. He needed to know how far she'd go with him, if she'd be willing to shed every inhibition on a whim.

Alexis entwined her arms around his neck, crushing her breasts against his chest. Softness to hardness. Heartbeat to heartbeat. Her fingers slid into the hair at the nape of his neck, her thumbs gently massaging the taut muscles there.

"I'll do anything," she said in a husky whisper. *"And everything…"*

Dear Reader,

May 2001 marks the celebration of the Get Caught Reading campaign, a national promotion created by North American publishers to encourage reading for the sheer joy of it. Books can take you into totally different worlds—worlds where the good guys always win, where love conquers all and where even the most unattainable fantasy can be fulfilled. And speaking of fantasies...

Welcome to FANTASIES INC., a place where your deepest desires can be satisfied. *Seductive Fantasy* is one of four lush island resorts that cater to provocative requests, which suits Jackson Witt's purpose just fine since he's got seductive revenge in mind. Alexis Baylor is looking to *be* seduced, but little does she know the gorgeous stranger who pursues her is more than an innovative lover. Both indulge in erotic pleasures and sensual adventures that leave them wanting more than they'd originally bargained for, but what happens when Jackson's true identity—and fantasy—is revealed?

Don't miss the upcoming books in the miniseries—*Secret Fantasy, Intimate Fantasy* and *Wild Fantasy.* Each will transport you to a private world full of decadent possibilities. In the meantime, I'd love to hear what you think of *Seductive Fantasy.* You can write to me at P.O. Box 1102, Rialto, CA 92377-1102, or at janelle@janelledenison.com.

Do you *have a secret fantasy?*

Janelle Denison

SEDUCTIVE FANTASY
Janelle Denison

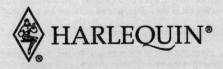

HARLEQUIN®

TORONTO • NEW YORK • LONDON
AMSTERDAM • PARIS • SYDNEY • HAMBURG
STOCKHOLM • ATHENS • TOKYO • MILAN • MADRID
PRAGUE • WARSAW • BUDAPEST • AUCKLAND

To Don.
You're living proof that fantasies do come true.
This one is for you alone.

ISBN 0-373-25932-8

SEDUCTIVE FANTASY

Copyright © 2001 by Janelle Denison.

This edition published by arrangement with Harlequin Books S.A.

® and TM are trademarks of the publisher. Trademarks indicated with ® are registered in the United States Patent and Trademark Office, the Canadian Trade Marks Office and in other countries.

Visit us at www.eHarlequin.com

Printed in U.S.A.

_____Prologue_____

ALEXIS BAYLOR wanted to have an affair and conceive a baby, and Merrilee Schaefer-Weston would do her best to accommodate the other woman's request. Merrilee's business was, after all, all about fulfilling her guests' fantasies.

"Ms. Weston, the seaplane is due to land at Seductive Fantasy in half an hour. The express boat is ready to take you to the island to greet our arriving guests."

Merrilee glanced up from reviewing Alexis Baylor's fantasy requisition papers and smiled at her assistant. Fantasies, Inc. encompassed a cluster of four lush paradise resorts off the Florida Keys. While her main office was situated on Wild Fantasy, the first of four island retreats, she traveled daily via boat to the other three themed resorts: Seductive Fantasy, Intimate Fantasy and Secret Fantasy.

"Thank you, Danielle." She glanced at her wristwatch, noting the time. "I'll be at the dock in ten minutes." Before her assistant turned to leave her office, Merrilee asked, "By the way, has personnel hired another pilot to replace Mark?"

"Yes, they have." Danielle thumbed efficiently through her notes on the clipboard she carried. Her finger came to a stop halfway down the page. "Here he is. C. J. Miller is slated to take over Mark's position next month, as scheduled."

Miller. As always when Merrilee encountered the very common last name, a head-to-toe chill swept through her, along with a flood of bittersweet memories of being young and head over heels in love. Those beloved recollections of her soulmate hadn't faded one iota over the thirty-five years that had passed between her romantic love affair with Charlie Miller, his unexpected and devastating death in Vietnam, and her marriage of convenience to a man twenty-three years older than her.

Merrilee had struggled through the lonely years that ensued, being a dutiful, faithful spouse to a cold, unemotional man who treated her more like a possession than a wife. She hadn't even had the luxury of having children to fill her life with joy; her husband's impotence had prevented that.

Upon his death five years ago, she'd inherited millions—more money than she'd ever realized Oliver was worth. She'd never enjoyed the role of pampered wife and couldn't imagine spending the rest of her life languishing in a mansion. And so, Fantasies, Inc. was born.

It might be too late for her to find ultimate happiness, but she'd decided to use her inheritance to fulfill other people's fantasies. She lived vicariously through the pleasure and satisfaction they discovered while on her island resorts. There was no fantasy—be it romance, adventure, or deeper desires that bared one's soul—that Fantasies, Inc. couldn't provide.

Never in her wildest dreams would she have believed her concept and themed island resorts would be so hugely, phenomenally successful.

"Ms. Weston?"

The distant voice of her assistant effectively pulled Merrilee back to the present. She blinked, shook the past from her mind, and focused in on the concern etching Danielle's features. "I'm sorry, what were you saying?"

The young woman tipped her head, regarding her curiously. "We were talking about the new pilot, C. J. Miller."

This time, Merrilee kept her thoughts firmly grounded and on business. "C. J. Miller. Right," she murmured, jotting down the name—as if she could forget it—and the date the man was scheduled to take over Mark's position.

"I'll go tell the boat driver you'll be at the dock shortly." With a swish of her perky ponytail, Danielle turned and left the office.

With only a few minutes to spare, Merrilee picked up the fantasy request she'd been pondering before her assistant's interruption. Alexis Baylor wanted to be desired and pursued by a gorgeous, sexy man, and hoped to conceive a baby with no strings attached; the man's involvement would stop there. While it would be easy to find a man eager to accommodate Alexis's request for a hot, erotic, one-week liaison, this particular fantasy had lifetime repercussions Merrilee doubted the woman had considered in her quest to fill that empty void in her life. Happily-ever-afters were Merrilee's specialty, and she always tried to give her clients two choices at the end of their fantasies—either walk away and continue as they were before, or take a risk that could reshape their whole entire life.

Merrilee drummed her manicured fingernails on her desktop and noted the date of Alexis's fantasy vacation. Though she couldn't guarantee conception—only fate could assure that—she had a month to figure out the woman's perfect match and donor. A man who'd fit both Alexis's and Merrilee's criteria. For Alexis, a man in his prime, both physically and sexually, who would seduce her single-mindedly. For Merrilee, a man who'd never shirk his responsibilities should he learn the truth. A man of integrity who'd ultimately fight for what was his. *If* that's how this particular fantasy played out.

All Merrilee could do was bring two matched souls together...it was up to the couple to grasp the happily-ever-after within their reach.

1

"DAMN THAT Alexis Baylor," Jackson Witt muttered beneath his breath.

Four years ago, Jackson vowed he'd never allow another woman to dupe him. That Alexis Baylor, a complete stranger, had managed to accomplish that feat not only made him feel like a fool, but also incensed him beyond reason. He was certain that sensation wouldn't abate until this whole aggravating mess was over. And it would be...just as soon as he discovered Alexis Baylor's greatest weakness and used it against her. Just as she'd used him.

The woman's underhandedness had hit him professionally as well as personally—right at the heart of his company, Extreme Software. He was still reeling from the knowledge that Fred Hobson, a man he'd hired on as part of his design team, had been a plant to steal the secret technology Jackson had spent years perfecting. The man had abruptly quit nine months ago and was conveniently and immediately picked up by Gametek, the company Fred had *previously* worked for before hiring on with Jackson's firm. Gametek had obviously wasted no time utilizing Extreme Software's design.

In Jackson's opinion, and with the facts he had at his disposal, it was no coincidence that the proprietary code Gametek had used in their new, revolutionary gaming software matched his exactly, or that Alexis Baylor, owner of Gametek, was a ruthless businesswoman who'd stooped to piracy to obtain success.

With a disgusted grunt, Jackson tossed aside the Business Wire he'd printed from the Internet a week ago—his first shocking insight into Gametek's violation. The company's press release announced that their innovative action-adventure game, *Zantoid*, compliments of *his* technology, was scheduled for market introduction that fall. Seemingly overnight, Gametek, a San Diego-based gaming software company Jackson had never heard of before this fiasco, was suddenly a big competitor. After Gametek's public statement, their stock shot to an all-time high and was holding steady...and would plummet to an all-time low by the time Jackson was done with Gametek, and Alexis Baylor.

The stakes were personal, an unwelcome reminder of how women always wanted something from him, from his own mother to the ladies he dated. Usually it was his money and what it could buy that women found so attractive, and while Alexis Baylor didn't have a direct hand in his wallet, she sure as hell had a direct source to his financial gain. He'd worked too damned hard to build his company, struggled through too many lean years to allow this woman to reap the benefits of something that was his.

Glancing at the clock on the wall in his office, he noted the time of 8:50 a.m. He had another ten minutes before Mike Mansel arrived. Mike was his best friend, as well as the private investigator Jackson had hired for an in-depth, confidential report on Alexis Baylor. He wanted specific details on the woman, from what she ate for breakfast, to whom she was seeing, to what she did in her leisure time, and every idiosyncrasy, no matter how mundane, Mike could discover.

Feeling edgy and impatient, Jackson pushed away from his desk and stood. He paced in front of the floor-to-ceiling windows dominating one entire wall in his Atlanta high-rise office, but the movement did little to burn his restless energy.

He'd already discussed with his attorneys about filing a complaint alleging copyright infringement, unfair competition, trade secret violations, and a bunch of other legal mumbo jumbo, which included seeking an injunction against Gametek to keep their software from hitting the market while they battled specifics in court. While his lawyers explored all legal possibilities against Gametek, Jackson craved personal compensation—a way of evening the score between himself and Alexis Baylor.

He wanted to take something from her, just as she'd stolen from him, something private and emotional that would never allow her to forget who he was, and what she'd done. He refused to let yet another woman use him for her own gain and get away with the deed. The type of information Mike unearthed on Alexis would determine Jackson's plan.

"Mr. Witt," his young secretary's lilting voice

drifted through the intercom on his desk, "Mike Mansel is here to see you."

Anticipation swelled within Jackson, chasing away the more frustrating emotions that had been his constant companions for the past week. "Thank you, Rachel. Send him back to my office and hold my calls until he leaves."

"Yes, sir."

The line disconnected, and less than a minute later Mike, dressed casually in jeans and a polo shirt, sauntered into Jackson's office in his normal, easy-going manner. Despite his carefree attitude, Mike was a highly respected P.I. Jackson had not only trusted him implicitly as a friend since their college days, but regarded him as a discreet businessman as well.

Mike set his scuffed leather briefcase on a clear spot on the corner of the solid oak desk, and Jackson reached across the distance to shake his friend's hand in greeting before sitting down in his chair.

"Thanks for making this case a priority," he said, knowing how abrupt his request for Mike's services had been.

The other man shrugged off his gratitude. "You can express your appreciation by buying me a cold beer sometime. Seems I owe *you* for all the business you've sent my way."

Mike was one of the few people who didn't expect anything from him but friendship, so it was extremely easy to promote him and his P.I. agency. "You don't owe me anything, Mike, and your fee will be in the mail by the end of the day. Now, what've you got for me on Alexis Baylor?"

"Not much other than a normal, predictable, everyday schedule and some background facts that don't add up to anything illegal or disreputable, personally *or* professionally." Mike sprawled his long, lean body into one of the beige leather chairs in front of the desk. "Sorry to disappoint you, Jackson. The woman is so damn clean she squeaks."

Jackson knew better than to believe Alexis was completely guileless and led an exemplary life free of any infractions or misdeeds. Not after he'd discovered she'd used one of her own as a mole to unearth secret information from his company.

A wry smile tipped the corner of his mouth. "Maybe that's because she depends on someone else to do her dirty work."

"That may be," Mike conceded, "but I spent five solid days of surveillance and gathering information on her, trying to find something to lend credence to your claim that this woman is ruthless, and I'm telling you, there's nothing remotely unscrupulous about her that I could discover."

"Consider her a good actress, because I have Gametek's press release that states otherwise. She stole my technology through Fred Hobson, and I want to even the score." He tapped his pen on his blotter impatiently and rerouted them back to the business at hand before his friend could argue further. "Tell me what you *did* find on her."

Mike stared at him for a long moment, then opened his briefcase, pulled out a file folder and withdrew a sheaf of papers stapled neatly together. "It's all in my report, but I'll give you a brief rundown."

He tossed the typed summary in front of Jackson to read while he went on to recite the facts by memory. "Alexis Baylor's parents died when she was ten, and her uncle, being the only family she had, raised her. Martin Baylor never married and devoted his time to his company, Gametek, which never took off while he was alive. From all accounts, Alexis was a quiet, shy girl and followed in her uncle's line of work. She attended San Diego State University, majored in Computer Science, and graduated at the top of her class. She went straight to work for her uncle designing basic computer games. When he died three years ago, she inherited the company."

Jackson dragged a hand over his clean shaven jaw. "How convenient," he drawled.

Mike shrugged off his comment. "Alexis was Martin's only family, too, so there really was no one else to take over the business. She didn't inherit much in the way of wealth, considering the company was near bankruptcy. From what I learned from other sources she's been working on *Zantoid* for the past four years, but hadn't been able to market the software because it was lacking a specific proprietary code to make the game run smoother, faster, and make the graphics more vibrant and real."

"*My* proprietary code," Jackson interjected through gritted teeth.

"Yes," Mike admitted with a pained half-smile. "There's no denying that the code is yours, or that she's reaping the benefits of your technology. She's received hundreds of thousands of orders for the software since announcing its release."

Jackson's gut twisted with aggravation. Exhaling a taut breath, he waved a hand in the air between them, as if the gesture alone could dismiss that disturbing news just as easily. "Go on with your report," he said, desperately needing to grasp onto something concrete about the woman he could use to his advantage. "What do you know about Alexis's personal life?"

Reclining in his chair in a deceptively lazy stretch, Mike folded his hands over his stomach and rested one sneakered foot over the opposite knee. "She actually goes by the name of Alex. She just turned twenty-eight and has never been married. She dates occasionally, but hasn't had a steady boyfriend in the past five years. Though Dennis Merrick, the man she promoted to vice president of the company after her uncle's death, seems very fond of her."

The woman hadn't had a steady boyfriend in the past five years? Jackson frowned, wondering why, and latched onto the most plausible explanation. "Is there something going on between her and her VP?"

Mike shook his head. "No. From what I could find out, he's been with the company for over ten years and was her uncle's right-hand man so it was a logical promotion to VP. She seems to depend on him for support and decision making and while he appears to be a good friend she spends occasional time with outside of the office, the interest is very one-sided."

Nothing to exploit there, Jackson thought in grow-ing dissatisfaction.

"She's very plain and unassuming," Mike contin-ued with his findings. "She spends her days at the office, goes out to a nearby deli for lunch, usually alone and with a book. She reads romantic suspense, in case you're wondering," he added with a grin. "She orders the same thing every day, a chicken salad sandwich, a side compote of fresh fruit and an iced tea with two lemons. She works at the office un-til nine or ten at night, and when she leaves for the evening she heads straight home to her two-bedroom condo in San Diego. Always alone."

Jackson winced at the woman's dull and boring social life. Mike's profile of Alexis didn't even come close to matching the vixen-like vision he'd conjured in his mind. "Are we talking about the same woman here?"

Mike laughed, but his humor quickly faded away. "I don't know what to tell you, Jackson. If the woman has an unscrupulous side, immoral habits or condemning fetishes, she hides them well. Her two biggest indulgences in the week that I had her under surveillance were a box of Amaretto truffles, and a few silky, lacy underthings she bought for herself at a lingerie boutique. Other than that, the woman is as straight as an arrow."

Jackson snorted at that, remembering how he'd to-tally and completely misjudged his fiancée, too. How easily she'd deceived him with outward ap-pearances and practiced affection. On the surface she'd presented the facade of a devoted and loving woman who catered to his every need and made him believe they were matched physically as well as intellectually. The kind of lifetime mate he could trust and build a life with. And then he'd discovered the deeper, scheming motivations she'd had for wanting to marry him. It had been a very nasty, public breakup four years ago, one that had made him keep women at arm's length ever since.

Looking back on the relationship, Jackson now realized he'd played right into Lindsay's ploy. He'd wanted to believe she'd share in the kind of emotional intimacy and trust that had always been missing from his life, things he'd secretly desired for years but had come to accept he'd never have. His own mother had never provided emotional nurturing and unconditional love, then had completely abandoned him when he'd been a teenager. She'd traipsed back into his life years later when he'd become a successful businessman, pretending love and adoration and begging forgiveness. The little boy in him wanted so badly to believe that she'd changed that he'd allowed her back into his life, until it became painfully apparent that she, too, was only interested in his money. He was merely another person in a long line of fools she'd used for her own purposes.

He wasn't one to hold onto grudges, yet every time he tried to let go of the past and let down his guard enough to trust someone and build a relationship, he was blindsided by ulterior motives and betrayal. It was safer, easier and less painful not to allow another woman that close.

Jackson rubbed his thumb along his chin, trying to ignore the churning in his belly those memories evoked. "What does Alexis look like?" he asked, tossing aside the thoughts of those two self-centered women for the current one wreaking havoc with his life.

"I was wondering when you were going to ask that question." A slow grin eased up the corners of Mike's mouth. "She's certainly nothing spectacular or anything like the sophisticated beauties you're used to dealing with. Definitely not the kind of woman who'd turn your head twice if you passed her on the street. Her features are pretty, but plain, and while she wears loose, unfitted clothing it's fairly obvious that she has *real* womanly curves beneath all that camouflage."

Leaning forward, Mike rifled through the contents of his briefcase and pulled out a manila envelope. From that, he withdrew an 8x10 glossy photograph and held the snapshot across the desk for Jackson to take. "I used my zoom lens to get a close-up of her for you. There are other shots in the envelope you can look through later."

Jackson examined the candid picture through critical eyes. The photograph had been taken as she was leaving her office building midday, accompanied by a thirty-something, brown-haired man with wire-rimmed glasses. First, Jackson focused on Alexis. As Mike had divulged, her looks and appearance were plain and unassuming and nothing remotely close to what Jackson had imagined. Minimal makeup enhanced her features and her glossy black hair was pulled back into one of those French braids. She wore an untucked, loose navy blue blouse that hinted at generous breasts but didn't fully display them, and a flowing patterned skirt that swirled around her legs and ankles.

Despite the unflattering clothing, he couldn't stop himself from envisioning the satiny, lacy underthings she might be wearing beneath the practical, unflattering outfit. He imagined warm, soft skin against cool silk, and a flush of unexpected heat infused him. Annoyed with his response, he immediately shook those unbidden thoughts right out of his head.

Sophisticated and extraordinarily beautiful, she wasn't. But he didn't doubt Alexis's intelligence. She was laughing at something the other man must have said, and her eyes, a pale but sparkling shade of blue, seemed to say "I'm at the top of the world".

Of course she was sitting pretty...she was in the position to make millions from all *his* hard work.

"Who is the guy with her?" Jackson asked curiously.

"That's Dennis Merrick."

Jackson looked once more. No, they didn't seem like lovers in the picture. Alexis appeared more amused by the man than enamored. But there was no denying the wistfulness in the other man's expression as he gazed at her.

Setting the photo aside, Jackson indicated the report and pinned his friend with an unrelenting stare. "You do realize, don't you, that you've given me nothing substantial to work with here."

"What can I say, other than sometimes that happens." Mike's tone held a silent apology as he stood and closed his briefcase. "I can only give you information that's available. I dug as deep as I could on Alexis Baylor, and while I have no doubt she stole your design, I couldn't find anything personally incriminating on her."

And that put Jackson back on square one and without a way of exacting personal retribution from Alexis as he'd hoped. "I know you did your best," he acknowledged, still confident in Mike's abilities, but disappointed nonetheless. "Thanks for your time and work on this case. I'll catch you later for that cold beer."

"I'm holding you to it." Lifting his briefcase from the desk, Mike turned to go, then swung back around, his head tipped to the side. "I forgot to mention something. It's in my report, but just so you know, Alexis is leaving this Saturday for a weeklong vacation."

That snagged Jackson's attention and he shuffled past the photo of Alexis and her VP to the summary Mike had given him. "To where?" he asked as he thumbed anxiously through the pages for the information he was sure Mike would supply.

"A place called Seductive Fantasy."

Jackson glanced up sharply, certain his expression reflected his incredulity. "What the hell is Seductive Fantasy?"

"Believe it or not, it's one of four island resorts off the Florida Keys that caters to people's fantasies—for a price, of course."

Jackson's jaw opened, snapped shut, then he shook his head in disbelief. "You're joking, right?"

Mike had to be. He'd never heard of anything so ridiculous. So *intriguing*.

"I checked it out. Fantasies, Inc. is legit, and so is Alexis Baylor's reservation."

Which put a whole different spin on Jackson's quest for personal revenge. "What's Alexis's fantasy?"

"All fantasies are confidential."

"There has to be some way to find out—"

Mike held up a hand, stopping his tirade. "I called the resort directly. Trust me, Merrilee Schaefer-Weston, the woman who owns the place, is a stickler about confidentiality. And I can't blame her, considering that she's dealing with people's deepest, most private secrets and desires. But it is a fascinating concept, don't you think?"

"Very fascinating," Jackson murmured, feeling a rush of excitement as he realized how Alexis's fantasy vacation could work to his advantage as well. Anonymity. Close proximity. *His* fantasy. Could getting to Alexis truly be as easy as filling out paperwork, paying a fee and stepping into a role that would enable him to walk away the victor this time?

He managed, just barely, to tamp his exhilaration. "Is she going to this island with anyone?"

Mike shifted on his feet and reluctantly divulged more. "It's a single seat reservation, so I'm assuming she's going alone."

"Perfect."

Understanding dawned across Mike's face. "I take

it you have a fantasy of your own to request from Ms. Weston?"

Jackson gave him a smug smile. "I believe I do."

Mike frowned. "I know you're upset, but doing something like this is so unlike you."

"What can I say?" Jackson said without a trace of an apology. "Alexis Baylor put my business and livelihood at stake. I'm tired of being used by women with agendas. This time I'm doing something about it."

"Be careful what you wish for, Jackson," he said in a low, cautioning tone of voice.

Jackson's deep laughter filled his office. "Why? Because I might just get what I ask for?"

"Exactly. For as intriguing as I find this fantasy stuff, I can't help but think that there are things and outcomes a person can't factor in when they wish and pay for something that doesn't come naturally." He shrugged. "It's like messing with fate."

Or maybe this whole setup *was* fate. Jackson rocked back in his chair, refusing to allow his friend's warning to deter him, no matter how logical Mike's comment was. "That's your suspicious P.I. nature talking, Mansel." After all, what could go wrong?

"Maybe," he acknowledged, but clearly wasn't done expressing his concern. "You'll probably get your revenge against Alexis Baylor in the guise of some other fantasy, but you might want to consider that the cost could be a personal one for you, too."

Jackson rolled his shoulders, trying to shake off the premonition of doom Mike was conjuring up.

He'd already paid personally because of Alexis Baylor, and couldn't imagine walking away from that fantasy resort after a week's time any worse off than he already was. "That's a risk I'm more than willing to take." His tone rang with finality.

"Well, good luck, then." Mike's chest expanded as he inhaled a slow, deep breath. Then one of his easygoing smiles graced his mouth. "Call me when you get back, and we'll have that beer together."

"And celebrate the success of my fantasy," Jackson added.

Once Mike was gone and Jackson was alone, he contemplated the situation and what had so unexpectedly fallen into his lap. Before he called Fantasies, Inc., he needed to figure out what kind of revenge he wanted against Alexis—not that he'd give Merrilee Schaeffer-Weston any insight to his *real* fantasy. The other woman would ban him from her resort if she knew his true intentions, and rightly so. No, it was imperative that Merrilee believed his motivations for requesting a fantasy were sincere.

He only had a few days to put his plans into motion. Once his fantasy was set up, Jackson decided he would give his attorneys permission to go forward with the lawsuit, the day before Alexis was due to leave on her vacation to Seductive Fantasy. Alexis would be aware of the impending lawsuit as well as the name of Extreme Software, but most likely wouldn't have the time to uncover specifics, such as who Jackson was, until he divulged the truth at the end of *his* fantasy. In a week's time, when he returned, he could follow through with court dates and appearances. And every time she'd see him during the trial he'd accumulate another personal victory, because she'd have to face him day after day.

He glanced at the picture Mike had taken and remembered what his friend had said: she hasn't had a steady boyfriend in the past five years. He didn't know the reasons, and in the scheme of things it didn't really matter.

He'd just chosen his private, personal fantasy.

He wanted plain and single Alexis to fall hard and fast and deeply for him. No woman could resist an out-and-out romantic pursuit. And in the end, once he knew he'd ensnared her emotions, he'd walk away with the knowledge that he'd stolen something integral from *her*.

Her heart.

2

DON'T LOOK OUT the window and you'll be just fine.

Alexis Baylor chanted that litany over in her mind as the small seaplane started its ascent from Miami for the fifteen minute flight to Seductive Fantasy off the Florida Keys. Keeping her eyes closed since boarding the compact aircraft, Alex now forced herself to take deep, even breaths to ease her anxiety as the plane scaled higher and higher. Her entire body felt the building velocity, and the buzzing sound of the engine seemed to rattle her bones. Despite her best efforts to remain calm, her stomach insisted on gauging even the most subtle dips they encountered during their upward climb.

Relax, relax, relax...

Her muscles remained tense; her heart beat triple-time. Alex never believed she harbored a fear of flying. In fact, her flight from San Diego to Miami had gone smoothly and remarkably well, without any incidences or panic attacks. Sitting in first class and being surrounded by luxurious leather seats while listening to a soft jazz station on the supplied headset, she'd been lulled by the comfort and security of being in a big, sturdy jetliner. But the moment she'd stepped aboard the Fantasies, Inc. commuter plane, an acute case of apprehension and claustrophobia had seized her, along with a flood of painful childhood memories that had a more profound effect on her than she'd realized.

Inhale, exhale, inhale, exhale...

Thankfully, the plane reached elevation and leveled out. Gradually, so did Alex's erratic pulse, but she knew better than to open her eyes and look out the window beside her. She had no desire to see the vast blue ocean below, or think about the awful last moments her parents must have spent together before their own private Cessna airplane had plummeted, taking them to their watery grave off the coast of San Diego.

She settled back into her seat as comfortably as her rigid body would allow, determined to keep her mind on other, more delightful matters for the duration of the flight...like the fantasy she'd bought and paid for and would soon experience. Yet even that exciting diversion was encumbered with troubling thoughts when she recalled how she'd nearly cancelled this trip at the very last minute.

Yesterday afternoon, to be exact. Right after her company had been served with an unexpected and disturbing complaint alleging copyright infringement and seeking an injunction against Gametek. The plaintiff, Extreme Software, claimed that it owned the proprietary code she'd used in her game and was filing a lawsuit to keep Gametek from marketing *Zantoid*. A hearing had been set for the week after she returned from her vacation. Her lawyers assured her it wasn't necessary for her to attend the proceeding, but she intended to go nonetheless and see for herself the parties who were suing her company—and trying to cash in on *her* success.

But until that court date, Dennis Merrick, the VP of her company, assured her that nothing would be gained by her calling off the trip she'd booked six months prior. He'd insisted she go, relax, and have a good time, and promised to handle the lawyers, investigations, and any legalities that might arise in her absence. As always, he made it more than clear that she could always count on him.

A wry smile touched the corner of her mouth. If Dennis knew the nature of the vacation she'd been saving toward for the past two years, ever since she'd read a magazine article about Fantasies, Inc., she was certain he wouldn't have been so supportive of her decision to leave. In fact, he would have been downright appalled. But his opinion made no difference. She knew what she wanted and nothing could change that. She wanted to be swept off her feet and seduced by a sexy man, no strings attached, and return home pregnant with the child she'd desired for years. A baby who would love her unconditionally and give her the sense of family she'd never really had.

Dennis would have gladly volunteered to fulfill her fantasy. Except she didn't want the complication of mixing their business relationship with something more intimate. There was also the important fact that she didn't connect with him on a physical and emotional level.

She'd known for years that Dennis harbored feelings toward her, but she'd always been careful not to lead him on or give him the wrong impression. She adored him as a friend, trusted him as an employee and respected him as a man. Dennis, for all his loyalty and obvious affection toward her, didn't make her feel breathless with excitement. No man ever had. Then again, she wasn't the type of sensual, sophisticated woman who inspired a man's intense, sexual interest. And since she'd recently come to the conclusion that she'd probably never experience the kind of passionate, impetuous, devoted relationship her own parents had shared, this fantasy would be her last chance to embrace all those lush, uninhibited, thrilling pleasures she'd been denied before she settled into motherhood. Alone and on her own.

In the meantime, with an attractive, enticing stranger picked out for her sole enjoyment and gratification, she'd wholeheartedly indulge in the feeling of being desired and desirable. She planned to drench every one of her five senses in the luxury of being romantically pursued.

Alex released a calm breath and shifted in her seat. Because of the personal, intimate nature of Alex's request, Ms. Weston had assured her that she'd do her best to make sure that her fantasy man would possess the same physical characteristics as she—black hair and blue eyes—so that there would be a much greater chance of conceiving a baby with her same traits.

Obviously, there was no promise that she'd leave with a child—only Mother Nature, not a paid fantasy, could guarantee that. But in five more days she'd be at her most fertile, and she planned to make the most of that opportunity.

Without warning, the plane hit an air pocket, and the cabin shook from the unexpected turbulence, jarring Alex out of the tranquility that had settled over her. She sucked in a sharp breath and her hand automatically shot out to grip the armrest between her seat and another passenger's. Instead of cushioned upholstery she came into contact with the firm, sinewy muscle of a man's arm. Hair roughened and incredibly warm and inviting, his skin disturbed her more than the aircraft's brief change in altitude.

Chagrined that she'd latched onto a stranger, a very masculine, athletically built stranger if that strong arm was any indication, she immediately snatched her fingers back and settled her balled up fists in her lap.

"Sorry," she murmured, keeping her eyes tightly closed, as if that could conceal her acute embarrassment. She might have been able to hide her eyes but there was nothing she could do to disguise the obvious heat spreading up her neck, across her cheeks, and all the way to the tips of her ears. The burning sensation made her feel restless in a way she didn't fully understand.

Before she could contemplate her startling reaction, long fingers grazed lightly across her clenched knuckles, and her pulse skyrocketed. Someone, the man she assumed was sitting beside her, picked up her hand, drew it across the armrest separating them, and slowly and gently unfurled her fingers. She swallowed, hard, as he flattened her hand between two incredibly large palms, engulfing her in a strange mixture of heat and soothing comfort. She'd been alone for so long, she couldn't recall the last time she'd experienced such a tender gesture.

He swept his thumb along the veins in her wrist, then pressed it against her rapid, erratic pulse. "Your heartbeat is unsteady. Are you okay?"

His voice was smooth and rich, like the decadent Amaretto truffles she indulged in on occasion. Spirals of awareness curled through her, wreaking havoc with the feminine nerves that had lain dormant for too long. Unable to speak for a variety of reasons, most prominent of which was her response to him, she nodded jerkily.

"Then open your eyes and look at me so I can see for myself that you're okay," he coaxed in that deep, delicious tone.

For the first time since boarding the seaplane, she lifted her lashes...and stared into a dark, velvet blue gaze that made her own blue eyes pale in comparison. Her stomach dipped, and this time being thrown off balance had nothing to do with the plane hitting an air pocket, and everything to do with the man sitting next to her.

He was big, solidly male and gorgeous in a way that made her feel extremely self-conscious of her own ordinary features. For the sake of comfort during her long ten-hour trip to Florida, and admittedly, out of routine, she'd twisted her hair into a French braid to keep it neat and tidy, and had worn a comfortable loose skirt and blouse to travel in. Never in her entire life had she been more aware of her appearance...and how frumpy she must look.

"That's better." A charming grin lifted the corners of his mouth. "At least now I'm assured that you're not going to pass out on me."

No, but she was feeling a bit light-headed from all this attention. She struggled to find her voice. "I'll be fine...just as soon as we land."

"Which can't be soon enough for you, I take it?"

She shook her head and laughed, the sound strained with nerves and the kind of tantalizing awareness she wasn't used to feeling. "No. The sooner the better."

His hair, she noticed, was cut into a neat, executive-type style that accentuated his handsome, chiseled features. The thick strands were an inky black, and a perfect complement to her own ebony mane. So far, he had the makings of her own personal fantasy man.

A staggering excitement rushed through her blood at the thought, though she couldn't be certain that he was *the one*. He could be just as he presented—a gentleman assisting a woman in distress. And most likely he was exactly that.

He tipped his head, regarding her curiously. "Are you afraid of flying?"

"Sort of," she admitted. "My parents died in a small plane just like this one."

"Aah," he said in understanding, giving her hand a gentle, compassionate squeeze that tugged at something equally elemental within her. "I'm sorry."

"It was a long time ago." She rested her head against the back of her seat, keeping her gaze averted from the window. "I was only ten at the time, but being closed in and flying over the ocean brings back memories of how they passed away."

"Understandably so," he murmured.

Realizing he still held her hand between his, and sure he'd rather let her go but was being polite, she attempted to withdraw from his grasp. He held her captive, his hold firm, his fascination with her undeniably genuine. Pressing her splayed fingers against a taut, denim-covered thigh, he lightly trapped her hand beneath the press of his palm.

As if she was going anywhere!

Absently, he stroked the skin between her thumb and forefinger, the caress so intimate and sensual it made her quiver deep inside. "Maybe I can help keep you distracted for the remainder of the flight."

Oh, she was most definitely distracted...and mesmerized. His sole focus was on her, which was beguiling in itself.

"I suppose we should start with introductions," he said, another lazy, sexy smile making an appearance. "I'm Jackson Witt. And you are?"

Completely smitten. Alex supposed that's what happened when a woman was the focal point of a gorgeous man's attention. She'd dated a handful of men, one long enough in college to constitute a relationship, but none had ever made her feel so entranced and infatuated at first glance.

She noticed the suddenly intense way he was staring at her, as if he was waiting for some kind of reaction. Well, she was definitely affected by him, except there was no way for him to see the internal flurry of rippling heat and sultry desire he evoked.

She called up a reciprocating smile that she found came easily to her lips. "It's nice to meet you, Jackson," she said, and was taken aback by the visible relief that passed across his expression. It was gone so quickly, she had to wonder if she'd imagined the odd emotion. "I'm Alexis Baylor, but everyone calls me Alex."

"Why?" he asked abruptly.

She shook her head in confusion. "Why what?"

"Why does everyone call you Alex when Alexis is such a beautiful name?"

She ducked her head, contemplating his comment. Honestly, she'd never felt much like an Alexis, a name which to her implied elegance and grace.

Slanting him a glance, she shrugged, having long ago grown used to the boyish nickname. "My uncle, who raised me after my parents passed away, always called me Alex, and I suppose it became a habit."

He grinned with sinful intent, his blue eyes sparkling mischievously. "One I intend to break... *Alexis.*"

The way her name rolled off his tongue was like a silky, sensual caress to her senses. Adding to that pleasant mental stimulation was the featherlight stroke of his fingers between hers, where she'd suddenly become ultrasensitive. While his touch was innocent, her entire body hummed with a luxurious warmth, one that was provocative as well as enjoyable.

"So, where are you from?" he asked.

She knew he was trying to make idle conversation, and she appreciated the diversion. "San Diego."

A dark brow winged upward. "Considering how uncomfortable you seem in a plane, how did you manage to get to Miami? By train?"

She laughed, and this time the sound was light and carefree, lacking the tension that had engulfed her earlier. "I flew, of course. It's the smaller commuter planes I have a problem with, not big, sturdy jetliners. And where are you from?"

"Atlanta."

She toyed with the end of her braid, which curled over her shoulder and rested just above her breast. "And I take it you're going to Seductive Fantasy, too?"

He nodded, his gaze shifting from the play of her fingers to her mouth, then her eyes, his perusal slow and lazy. "Yes."

So, he either had a fantasy or was someone's fantasy—or maybe both. "For a fantasy?" she asked, hoping the obvious question would unearth deeper information about the man.

His eyes darkened, turning a smokey shade of blue. "Most definitely for a fantasy," he murmured.

She shivered at the sudden intensity cloaking him. Unable to help herself, even though she knew she was venturing into private territory, she asked, "What is *your* fantasy?" Was that her voice that sounded so breathless?

Beneath her trapped hand, his muscles bunched, belying his relaxed expression. He sent her a chastising look, tempered with flirtatious charm. "Why, Ms. Baylor, shame on you. I believe that information is confidential, as is your fantasy. Unless you care to share yours first?" he invited.

Her skin flushed, at being so bold as to ask about something so intimate, as well as at the thought of divulging her own deepest desires. Not only did she not really know this man and his personal intentions on Seductive Fantasy, but she wanted her request to play out on its own accord, without planting any preconceived notions in another man's head. Though with him admitting that he had his own fantasy to explore at the island resort, she didn't hold out much optimism that they'd be paired as a couple.

She let out a regretful sigh. "No, I'd rather not share my fantasy, and I apologize for asking about yours."

"No apology necessary," he said sincerely. "I suppose the nature of this vacation retreat does stir one's imagination. I have to confess that I'm equally curious to know what you're looking for on Seductive Fantasy."

Unadulterated passion. Uninhibited desire. A father for my baby. She kept those secrets tucked away. "Let's just say I'm trying to cram a lifetime of missed opportunities into one short week."

He turned the hand resting on his thigh over and traced a long, tapered finger against her palm, tickling her skin and arousing her to a fever pitch at the same time. "Well, I hope all your fantasies come true, Alexis."

She stared into his compelling eyes, hopelessly lost in the sea of sensuality she saw shimmering in the depths. She licked her suddenly dry lips. "I hope so, too," she replied huskily.

He continued doing incredible things to her hand, her fingers. Subtle, yet provocative caresses that had her breathing deepening and her body softening against her seat. Despite her best efforts to remain immune to his alluring touch, her belly quivered and her breasts swelled against the lacy webbing of her bra. The man was very close to providing the unadulterated passion part of her fantasy—and she couldn't help but wonder if that was part of his plan, or merely just a coincidence.

"We've arrived at Seductive Fantasy." The voice of Mark, their pilot, drifted from the cockpit and into the cabin. "Please stay seated a moment longer, until the plane is secured and the door is unlatched."

Alex's eyes rounded in shock. "We're here?" she asked incredulously.

Jackson's chuckle vibrated with a wealth of amusement. "Yep. I think it's safe for you to look out your window now."

Trusting him, she glanced out the small portal, stunned to discover that they had, indeed, landed. Water lapped at the floats attached to the seaplane as they glided smoothly on the ocean. They were slowly drifting toward a wooden walkway extending from the white sand beach of a lush island. Beyond stood a gorgeous hotel designed with Mediterranean appeal, and surrounded by bright tropical plants. Excitement blossomed within her at the sight of such beauty and elegance—the backdrop for her personal fantasy.

"Incredible." She looked back at her companion, unable to stop her own laughter from bubbling up out of her. "I wasn't even aware of the plane descending."

He winked at her. "Then I guess I lived up to my promise to keep you distracted."

Oh, he'd definitely managed that. Her elation dwindled as reality made an uninvited appearance. So, his attention had been a ruse after all, to keep her mind off the short trek across the Atlantic. Of course. She'd been silly to think otherwise, even briefly.

"It was very nice meeting you, Alexis," he said, drawing her out of her disappointing thoughts. Lifting her hand, he brushed a featherlight kiss across her knuckles, then finally released her from his hold.

She immediately missed the warmth he'd generated. "Likewise," she replied.

Once the cabin door was open and they were free to exit the aircraft, they unbuckled their seat belts, along with two other female guests Alex hadn't realized were sitting across from them until that moment. The four of them stepped out onto the walkway, and Alex squinted against the late afternoon sun as two men unloaded their luggage. The women's bags were the first to appear and were tossed onto a brass cart. Jackson's suitcases were next.

"Right this way, sir," one of the employees instructed, and started down the walkway toward an older woman waiting at the end of the platform. Without a final backward glance at Alex, Jackson followed the other man.

Alex watched him go, and with each step he took that put distance between them, she grew more desperate to catch his attention again.

Just one more time.

"Jackson..." his name slipped from her lips before she could stop the impulse.

He turned around, inclining his head questioningly. "Yes?"

Now that she had his undivided attention, as well as the interest of the Fantasies, Inc. employees, what did she say?

"Thank you," she said, expressing the gratitude he deserved. Self-consciously, she smoothed a hand down the front of her skirt and summoned a smile. "You made the flight more bearable, as well as enjoyable."

"It was my pleasure," he drawled in a low, sexy voice any woman would find vastly appealing. No doubt, many women *had*. "Maybe we'll run into each other on the island." With a final wave, he turned back around and continued on.

Butterflies hatched in Alex's stomach, making her feel like a schoolgirl in the throes of a crush. And oh, what a wonderful feeling it was! "Yes, maybe," she whispered to his retreating back. *I certainly hope so.*

Once her luggage was secured on a separate cart, Alex followed her guide to the end of the walkway. The woman who'd greeted Jackson moments ago now turned a bright smile her way. They clasped hands, and Alex was instantly immersed in the other woman's warmth and hospitality.

"I'm Merrilee Schaefer-Weston," she said, introducing herself. "And please call me Merrilee. Welcome to Seductive Fantasy, Alex."

"Thank you. I'm thrilled to be here." Alex had known just by talking to the other woman on the phone that she cared a great deal about her clients and their requests, and she immediately liked Merrilee. The kindness and dedication she witnessed in her gaze gave Alex more proof that the woman was devoted to her business and making her guest's fantasies come true.

"The island is yours to do as you please, in whatever way it pertains to your personal fantasy," Merrilee continued, and Alex was certain Jackson had received the same commentary before he'd disappeared down the path leading to the hotel. "If there is anything I can do to make your stay more enjoyable, I'm only a phone call away." She indicated the pager clipped to the waistband of her taupe-colored slacks. "My guests and their comfort are my number one priority, and I'm available 24-7. Do you have any questions before your fantasy begins?"

"I do have one," Alex admitted, chewing absently on her lower lip. "How will I know who my fantasy man is?"

A knowing smile curved Merrilee's lips. "He'll be everything you asked for, maybe more. He'll pursue you and make his intentions known."

Relief swept over Alex. "That's good to hear, because I'm not real good at making the first move when it comes to the opposite sex."

"You won't have to." The assurance in Merrilee's voice rang strong and true. Then her expression softened perceptibly. "And if I might impart a few words of advice before your fantasy begins, I'd tell you to follow your heart, Alex. It might lead you places you've never been before."

Alex couldn't contain the shiver that coursed through her at Merrilee's statement.

Two hours after they parted ways, Alex sat on the patio of her opulent suite, watching the sun set over the horizon in brilliant shades of pinks, purples and oranges. She contemplated the other woman's pearls of wisdom, and found Merrilee's choice of words odd considering love and emotional commitment weren't a part of her fantasy. She was entering this fantasy with practical expectations, not unrealistic hopes for the future.

Still puzzled but now hungry, Alex went back inside her room and flipped through the menu for room service. She had decided to eat in her room tonight—even if that meant missing out on her first opportunity to get acquainted with her fantasy man. She was too tired to be engaging, too exhausted to even enjoy a flirtatious advance. And admittedly, she was still too wound up from her encounter with Jackson to give another man a fair chance. She'd be refreshed and ready for romance and adventure after a good night's sleep.

As she waited for her meal to arrive, she strolled back out to the balcony, wrapped her hands around the cool railing, and scanned the suites across from hers. She wondered which one was Jackson's, and if he was off enjoying his own fantasy...and with whom.

WITH TIKI TORCHES and moonlight illuminating his way, Jackson strolled from his private cottage on the beach along the curving walkway that wound around the resort's lavish pool area. Without a doubt, the island was ideal for romance, forbidden temptation and erotic trysts. Unfortunately, disappointment was his only companion after his late-night walk to burn off the restless energy that had consumed him since arriving on Seductive Fantasy that afternoon.

Thanks to Mike's help, Jackson had managed to discover Alexis's flight times and book himself a seat on the same shuttle to the island, a way of insuring that they met before they even arrived at the resort. After how exceptionally well his first encounter with her had gone, he'd been hoping to proceed with his romantic pursuit this evening, but she hadn't cooperated with his personal strategy. Much to his frustration, he hadn't run into her since they'd parted ways at the dock.

With a harsh sigh of dissatisfaction, he made his way toward the Players' Lounge, deciding that if he didn't find Alexis in the singles' club, he'd call it a night. He entered the establishment, sidled up to the bar, and ordered a Tom Collins. While he waited for his order, he searched the guests mingling in the lounge and the couples dancing to the tunes the band was playing, hoping to find a certain black-haired, blue-eyed woman.

"Looking for someone special?" a female voice asked.

Jackson turned on his stool and wasn't surprised to find Merrilee standing beside him at the mahogany and brass bar. During the day he'd seen her around the resort tending to her guests' comfort and needs. And checking up on the progress of her clients' fantasies, he assumed. "As a matter of fact, I am."

A knowing smile made its way to her lips. "Alexis Baylor, by chance?"

He stiffened in his seat, wondering how in the world she'd made that connection when he'd been so careful to keep his intentions to himself. "What makes you think I'm looking for her?" The bartender delivered his drink, and Jackson thanked the other man.

"It was just a guess." She tilted her head, regarding him through kind blue eyes. "My pilot told me that the two of you hit it off on the flight over from Miami, and I saw the interaction between you and Alexis at the dock."

He laughed, breaking up the tension that banded his chest. Seeing no harm in divulging the truth, he said, "An accurate guess, I admit." He took a long swallow of his cool, tangy drink and reached for the bowl of shelled peanuts on the counter. "I *was* looking for Alexis."

"Well, Ms. Baylor opted to eat dinner in her

room," Merrilee informed him. "At last account she was in bed for the night."

Jackson met Merrilee's gaze as he took another drink, trying to gauge why she was supplying him with so much personal information on Alexis. "Looks like my efforts at trying to find her tonight were futile then."

"But tomorrow is another day."

"So it is."

Merrilee hesitated for a moment, then said, "On your fantasy application and when we spoke on the phone before you booked your trip, you said you wanted to find a woman you could open up to and trust."

"Yes." He managed, just barely, to refrain from wincing as a twinge of guilt nudged him. The lie he'd fabricated for a believable and acceptable fantasy had been a necessity, one he wasn't exactly proud of considering how much he liked and respected Merrilee. But he'd been pushed too far by one woman too many, and in order to obtain what he truly wanted from Alexis Baylor, he had no choice but to hold tight to that pretense.

He continued. "My relationships with women have been...lacking. And I've been betrayed one time too many." That much was pure truth. "It's a novel concept to me to be able to trust a woman."

She gave a compassionate nod of understanding. "I did tell you that you'd have to see how your request played out once you were at the resort, that I couldn't guarantee that you'd find a woman who suited your fantasy."

He tossed a few peanuts into his mouth and chewed. "I remember."

"However, I did want to ask, how does Alexis fit your perception of the kind of woman you want to open up to and trust?"

Jackson nearly choked on his peanuts. Coughing, he washed down the snack with a huge gulp of his drink. If he wasn't mistaken, she was singling him out, and offering him exactly what he wanted—a direct link to Alexis, all based on their connection on the seaplane.

He regained his composure and clung to his pretense. "I've only met her once, but Alexis *could* be that woman." He stared Merrilee straight in the eyes. "I definitely want to get to know her better, but the question is, do I fit into her reason for being here at Seductive Fantasy?"

"I believe you could, very easily. But of course the decision to accept *you* will ultimately be up to Alexis."

If all went as he planned, Jackson didn't see that as a problem, not after the way Alexis had reacted so favorably to him on the seaplane. He'd use that attraction to his advantage. "So, how do I go about doing this?" he asked.

"Well, I can help you out a bit." She smiled mischievously. "As part of your fantasy, and Alexis's, I can give you complete access to her whereabouts at all times, day or night. A phone call to Stewart at the concierge desk will provide you with details and information on Alexis so you can keep track of her.

However, if I see that she isn't interested, the privileged information will discontinue."

"Fair enough." Jackson realized that Merrilee was attempting to act as matchmaker and trusted him with Alexis. He did his best to ignore the tightening in his gut and the little voice in his head making him question what he was going to do. "For starters, can I have her room number?"

"Room 305, in the main hotel," she supplied easily, then pressed her soft hand to his arm. "I hope she's the one who makes up for all those other women in your life."

Jackson forced a smile and held back the comment, *she's going to be added to the growing list*. Merrilee moved on to mingle with other guests, granting Jackson a reprieve. Tossing a tip for the bartender onto the counter, he left the Players' Lounge and followed the path toward the hotel to seek out Alexis's room for future reference.

He shook his head as the day's events filtered through his mind. His first evening on the island certainly hadn't turned out as he'd expected. Then again, if he was honest with himself, Alexis Baylor wasn't what he'd anticipated, either. Not at all.

The pictures Mike had taken of her had accurately depicted her physical attributes. What those candid snapshots *hadn't* captured was just how soft and lush her mouth looked, how smooth and luminous her skin appeared, or how expressive her blue eyes were. Despite her plain, reserved packaging, she possessed the potential to transform herself into a sensual beauty, but obviously wasn't aware of her appeal. He found that realization amazing, especially when he was accustomed to women using their looks to their advantage.

In the flesh, Jackson had discovered that this particular woman was a paradox. The fascinating bits of vulnerability and softness she'd displayed on the seaplane had clashed with the image of the ruthless businesswoman he'd conjured in his mind. She'd been far more demure and reserved than he'd visualized, and he was finding it difficult to mesh the two individual, contradictory impressions.

With a disgusted grunt at his own gullibility, he reminded himself that this woman had cheated him and his company. Regardless of her modesty when it came to men, she definitely took an aggressive approach in business.

An approach he fully intended to emulate for the next week. A gradual buildup of flattery and romance to something far more assertive, persuasive and single-minded—a combination most women found difficult to withstand. And Merrilee had offered him the perfect opportunity to make Alexis the center of his attention. He'd initially take the chase slow and easy. Tease her. Tempt her. Then ultimately seduce her.

Judging by the attraction that had sparked between them in the seaplane, he had a strong feeling that Alexis Baylor wouldn't be able to resist him. Pursuing her, and delving past all that reserve, wouldn't be difficult for him, either. Not when she intrigued him, aroused him even, with her contradictions.

Jamming his hands into the front pockets of his jeans, Jackson followed the pathway through an elaborate garden of exotic plants and flowers flanking the courtyard designed between two separate wings of the hotel. There were benches situated along the trail and pillars entwined with night-blooming jasmine, scenting the air with a drugging, seductive perfume. His steps slowed and he glanced up at the four stories of suites looming in front of him, counting three up and five across, pinpointing Alexis's room. The interior was dark, but she'd left the glass slider open to allow fresh air to slip inside. The diaphanous sheers covering the window billowed gently in the fragrant, sultry evening breeze.

He imagined her warm and soft in her bed, her breathing deep and even. Did she wear her hair down and free, or did she keep it neat and orderly even at night? She might dress practically in loose clothing, but he couldn't stop himself from wondering what she slept in—something silky and decadent as Mike had suggested during his investigative report, or nothing at all? A slow burn settled in Jackson's belly at the thought.

Soon, he'd find out.

Tomorrow, the seduction would begin.

3

IF HER FANTASY MAN was on the island he had yet to make an appearance, and half of her second day on Seductive Fantasy was nearly over.

Exhaling a breath of frustration, Alexis lifted her gaze from the romantic suspense novel she couldn't quite concentrate on. She scanned the guests lounging around the pool area and couples conversing at the swim-up bar who were obviously enjoying *their* fantasies, whatever they may be.

For the umpteenth time in the past hour since she'd eaten a light lunch at the outdoor café, she searched for a dark-haired man with blue eyes who would set his sights on her and make that all important first advance. A man like Jackson.

There were many men with her requested characteristics, but none showed her any interest other than a brief glance or cordial smile. While she wasn't sitting directly in the sun and had opted for the shade of a large palm tree because she burned much too easily, she couldn't be in more plain sight for her soon-to-be lover to find her.

She'd always been an extremely patient person, but suddenly discovered she was *very* antsy to move on to the next phase of her paid vacation. *Her fantasy.* Now that she was refreshed and rested, she was eager to taste the heat of passion, and anxious to experience the kind of tantalizing, rapturous sensations she'd only read about.

Shifting restlessly on the lounge chair, she stretched her legs and flicked her flowing skirt over her exposed knees and calves. She frowned, realizing just how *clothed* she was compared to the rest of the scantily clad women around her—realizing, too, just how much attention *they* were receiving in comparison.

Though she'd been conservative in selecting her attire since she was a teenager, and had never given fashion a second thought, Alex wondered if maybe she should have purchased more alluring clothing for this vacation. Her one secret indulgence was wearing pretty, lacy lingerie, but her seductive underwear was a moot point if her outerwear didn't attract a man's attention.

With a sigh, she ducked her head back to her book, seeing the words but not really reading them as her mind turned over different possibilities. Yes, maybe she needed to change her image and live impetuously for the week, especially at a private resort where no one she knew would see or judge her. She could be anything or anyone she wanted and enjoy the results of being carefree and impulsive with no consequences other than the ones she'd requested. She could be daring, take wild risks, then return home and resume her practical lifestyle, as well as deal with the messy lawsuit awaiting her.

If only her fantasy man would arrive so she could start her journey to self-discovery.

Out of the corner of her eye she caught a glimpse of someone heading across the far deck, down the short concrete steps, and toward the pool...toward *her*.

Automatically, she raised her gaze to gauge this next potential offering, and her breath caught in her throat as she watched Jackson Witt burn a path closer and closer to where she sat, his stride purposeful and confidently male. Hope and electric currents of excitement mingled, racing through her bloodstream at a rapid pace. Who needed to sit out in the sun when this man had the ability to heat her from the inside out?

He was wearing navy blue swimming trunks and a tank shirt that showcased his broad shoulders and tapered to a lean waist. His strong thighs were toned and muscled, his legs long and well defined. Everything about him was exceptional and sensual and utterly masculine. Everything about him thrilled her.

She jerked her eyes back up to his gorgeous face, wishing he wasn't wearing sunglasses so she could see his gaze and assess his intentions. Just when she was absolutely certain he would approach her, he stopped abruptly a few yards away. In one fluid motion that set the muscles in his arms and across his back rippling, he pulled off his shirt while toeing off his deck shoes at the same time. He tossed the balled up cotton onto a chaise, added his sunglasses to the top of the pile and, without a glance in her direction, he strode to the edge of the pool. Diving into the water with smooth, graceful precision, he began a series of laps.

She groaned in acute regret, silently chastised her wishful thinking, and returned her attention to her book and off the man that every other woman in the vicinity was ogling. It was fairly obvious that Jackson had forgotten all about her, while he'd starred in her dreams last night and had given her the incentive to venture out early this morning in search of her fantasy man.

He obviously wasn't *the one*, she thought, sighing in disappointment.

Ten minutes later, when he climbed out of the pool at the deep end near where she was sitting, Alex forced herself to keep her nose in her book, eyes downcast, and pretend complete absorption in her story. She refused to embarrass herself by gawking at his magnificent body as he sauntered past her chair.

He made it difficult for her to ignore him. Instead of returning to the chaise holding his shirt and sunglasses, she heard the soft, wet, pit-pat of footsteps, then watched his bare feet come into view beside her lounge chair. She swallowed, hard, as water dripped off him and pooled around his legs.

Now what did she do?

Before she could gather the fortitude to glance up and greet him with a polite smile that didn't give away her strong attraction to him, she was showered with droplets of water as he shook his upper body and damp hair like a wet dog.

She gasped and dipped her head lower as the moisture rained down upon her, surprised at his playfulness when it was the very last thing she would have expected from him. Despite her best efforts, she couldn't contain the spontaneous laughter that escaped her. "Hey, you're getting me all wet!"

He stopped shaking himself dry and waited until she finally looked up at him. "Am I?" He asked the question innocently, but his eyes, framed by black spiked lashes, blazed with blue fire and impudence.

She wasn't used to being on the receiving end of sexual innuendo, but his double meaning wasn't lost on her. If he was going to be so brazen, then so was she. She wanted to see just how far he intended to take things between them...a light, friendly flirtation, or something more intimate?

"Yes, you are," she replied boldly.

"Good." A smile filled with too much satisfaction graced his lips. "You were deliberately ignoring me."

She opened her mouth to issue a denial, then promptly shut it to rethink her strategy when she realized she'd been caught. "You ignored me first," she countered, setting her book on the glass-topped table beside her.

"I was hot and wanted to cool off." He stepped away for a second and dragged a nearby lounge chair over, keeping it aligned in the sun instead of joining her in the shade. Straddling the chair, he plopped down into the seat and finger combed his damp hair away from his chiseled features. "I would have asked you to join me, but you aren't exactly dressed for a swim."

She most definitely needed to do something about her attire, including buying a one-piece bathing suit that would flatter her curvaceous figure and attract the attention of a man like Jackson. "I burn easily, so what's the point of wearing a swimsuit if I'm not going to sit directly in the sun?"

"So you can get all wet," he said, his amused tone a bit on the naughty side.

Oh, he was bad. And very good. "Which usually leads to playing in the sun and getting burned."

"That's what sunscreen is for. And if you just don't like being in the sun, I've been told that there are a few secluded, shady lagoons here on the island that you can reserve for your own private pool party."

"Really?" she murmured, intrigued by the notion. Intrigued, too, by the subtle invitation dancing in his velvet eyes.

"Uh-huh," he replied, the sound rising up from his throat in a sexy, arousing rumble. "With waterfalls and hot springs and all kinds of other decadent luxuries."

He tempted her with his words. He enticed her with the promise she heard in his voice. He enthralled her...lying there in the sun like an Adonis, letting the warm rays worship his body and dry the moisture on his skin.

Unbidden, her gaze drifted to his flat stomach, and she experienced the inexplicable urge to glide her fingers along the droplets of water clinging to the dark trail of hair that whorled around his navel and disappeared into the waistband of his trunks. She wanted to touch the damp, slick flesh stretching taut across his chest, his arms...

"Can I get either of you anything to eat or drink?"

Startled by the intrusion of a third voice, Alex snapped out of her provocative daydream and found herself staring at a waiter dressed in black shorts and a crisp knit shirt. He smiled at her expectantly, pen poised over the pad of paper on his drink tray.

She cleared her throat, realizing that her mouth was very parched and she was suddenly very thirsty. It seemed lusting over a man's body tended to dry up the salivary glands. "I'll take a piña colada."

He jotted down her order. "And you, sir?"

"I'll take a Tom Collins, and a bowl of fresh fruit."

The waiter nodded. "Coming right up."

Once the other man disappeared in the direction of the outdoor bar, Jackson folded his arms behind his head and turned those intense, velvet blue eyes back on her. "So, are you enjoying your stay here so far?"

His tone was back to casual and amicable, and his mixed signals unbalanced her. He went from naughty to nice in the span of minutes, and she couldn't quite decipher which direction he was heading with her.

She played it cautiously. "It's only been a day, but what's not to enjoy about this resort and island? The amenities are fabulous, and the staff is wonderful." Tucking her legs to the side, she revealed, "It's been a long time, if ever, since someone has catered to my every whim as they do here."

He tipped his head inquisitively. "All work and no play?"

She smiled. "Yeah, something like that." For the past few years her sole focus had been designing *Zantoid* and making sure Gametek didn't fall into bankruptcy. Having fun hadn't been a priority. And now that she was finally on the verge of success, someone was attempting to squash her accomplishments.

"And is your fantasy playing out the way you thought it would?"

"Not exactly," she admitted truthfully. "But I'm hoping that will change soon." A light breeze blew, and she brushed back a wayward wisp of hair that had unraveled from her braid. Her skin tingled as he watched her every move. "How about your fantasy?"

"So far, so good." His light tone echoed his contentment.

"You're satisfied with your fantasy already?" She couldn't contain the disbelief that seeped into her voice, couldn't help but feel cheated that he was already enjoying his fantasy when hers had yet to begin.

His gaze connected with hers, and a slow, sinful grin transformed his entire expression. "No complaints yet," he drawled. "Though I have a feeling it's going to get more satisfying as the week progresses."

His comment dangled seductively between them, confusing her already overloaded senses where he was concerned. She wanted, *needed*, something concrete to claim him as her own for the week. A clear and indisputable cue that she wouldn't be infringing upon someone else's property if she followed through with her deepest desires to have *him*.

"Here you go," the waiter said as he returned with their orders. He handed her a white frothy drink topped with a skewer of pineapple, orange and a cherry, passed Jackson his Tom Collins, then set a wooden bowl of fresh, succulent fruit on the table between their two lounge chairs. "Enjoy your afternoon," he said, then was gone.

Jackson nudged the bowl of fruit he'd ordered in her direction. "Help yourself."

She shook her head as she stirred her straw in her thick drink. "I just ate lunch."

He lifted a dark brow. "Don't tell me that you're one of those women who counts calories and watches everything they eat," he teased.

She laughed softly. "If you saw me in a bathing suit, you'd know that I'm not."

Leisurely, he assessed her, from her shoulders all the way down to her ankles, but Alexis knew there wasn't a whole lot for him to see considering what she was wearing. "Women were made to be soft and curvy, not skin and bones."

She shivered, not entirely certain her chill had anything to do with the frozen concoction sliding down her throat. "You're one of the rare few who like their women with a little extra padding." At least in her experience.

He shrugged and popped a melon ball into his

mouth and chewed. "I suppose I am, and you're perfect."

Before she could stop the urge, she rolled her eyes at his lavish compliment, certain he was just being a gentleman. "As if you can tell with what I'm wearing."

"I have a great imagination, Alexis," he said as he plucked a few grapes from the stem and ate them. "You might have been wearing an unfitted blouse yesterday, but that cotton T-shirt you have on now outlines full breasts, the indentation of your waist, and despite how loose your skirt is, there's no doubt in my mind that you have nicely rounded hips and long, smooth legs..."

To her dismay, her nipples tightened as if he'd caressed them with more than just his eyes. A warm flush infused her cheeks, and she held up a hand to stop his arousing monologue. "I get your point."

"Good," he murmured, looking smug and confident.

After taking a long drink, he set his glass on the table and settled more comfortably against his reclining chair. Tucking his thumbs into the waistband of his swim trunks, he turned his face toward the sun and promptly closed his eyes to bask in the languorous warmth.

Giving him his time to relax, she reached over to the bowl of fruit and pilfered a strawberry. As she nibbled on the sweet, succulent berry, she scanned the guests around them and wondered about each one of them...where they came from, what they did, and what had prompted them to purchase a private fantasy.

She wondered all those things about Jackson, too, and while they'd agreed yesterday on the seaplane that divulging their individual fantasies was off-limits, they hadn't established any rules about sharing personal information. She already knew that he lived in Atlanta. She had nothing against revealing her occupation, or even bits and pieces of her life and lifestyle away from the resort.

Curiosity got the best of her, as did the hope that her question might give her a deeper insight to this man who appealed to her on so many different levels. "Jackson?"

"Hmmm?" He sounded drowsy, as if she'd interrupted his downhill slide into slumber.

She drew a deep breath, and asked, "What do you do for a living?"

One eye peeked open to look at her, then the second followed suit. He blinked lazily, belying the sudden tension that seemed to tighten his jaw. "Does it matter?"

So much for getting to know him better. She finished her strawberry, licked her bottom lip, and sighed. "No, I suppose it doesn't."

He sat up, and crooked a finger at her. "C'mere," he said, throwing her completely off guard with the request.

Uncertain of what he wanted, but undeniably curious, she leaned toward him, closing the distance between them. "What is it?"

Reaching out, he dragged his thumb along the corner of her mouth and over the fullest part of her lower lip. Her stomach tumbled and her heart rate accelerated. She felt the blazing heat of his touch, then the smear of something sticky on her skin and realized that she must have missed some of the juice from the strawberry.

"Got it," he said triumphantly, then brought his finger to his mouth and sucked off the bright red wetness staining the pad of his thumb. "Mmm. Sweet."

Her breath rushed out of her lungs, and she struggled to maintain her composure instead of melting into a puddle of desire right on the spot. "The, um, strawberries are very ripe."

He smiled and gave his finger one last lingering taste. "And so are you." As if he hadn't just stirred her soul and awakened forbidden longings, he reclined back on his chaise, appearing completely, frustratingly nonchalant.

"The one nice thing about this fantasy stuff is the anonymity that comes with it," he said, resuming their previous conversation. He rolled his head to the side and met her gaze. "Being anything or anyone you want. Following impulses without worrying about what anyone might say or think because no one knows any differently than what your fantasy dictates."

Surprised that his theory reflected her own earlier thoughts, she made no reply, curious to hear more of his analogy.

"My fantasy could be that I'd like to be a self-made millionaire, and if I was playing that part here on the island, then what I did for a living in real life wouldn't really match that part of my fantasy, now would it?"

He made perfect sense. She sipped her piña colada and hid a grin. "Somehow I doubt your fantasy is to be a self-made millionaire."

"But you don't really know for certain, do you?"

That gave her a moment's pause. "No, I don't," she admitted.

"And not knowing adds to the excitement of this whole fantasy element, doesn't it?"

The sexy, intimate rasp of his voice, his hooded gaze, did crazy things to her insides. Exciting, shivery, liquid kind of things. She couldn't deny the truth he was asking for. "Yes, it does."

The heat in his eyes increased by several degrees. "It's just as exciting for me, too."

Too many seconds to count passed as his words swirled with all kinds of promise between them. Then finally, slowly, he pushed to his feet and stood, stretching the kinks from his long, lean body. "Well, I guess I should be going."

"You're leaving?" Her disappointment rang clear in her voice.

He braced his hands on his hips and grinned. "I figured I've infringed on enough of your time."

Not nearly enough! "I..." *wish you were my fantasy man,* "...enjoyed talking to you."

"Me, too."

He walked away, and Alex realized she was right back where she'd started this morning. Frustrated and anxious...and now aroused by a man who wasn't even a part of her fantasy.

Great.

She watched Jackson slip on his shoes, scoop up his T-shirt, then slide his glasses back on. Unable to shake her own discontent, she sat up, grabbed her book and decided that it was time she spoke to Merrilee and found out when, exactly, *her* fantasy would begin.

Abruptly she stood, turned around, and in her haste to be on her way nearly collided with a firm wall of muscled chest. Jackson's chest. She took a surprised step back and jerked her gaze up to his face. "I thought you were gone."

Fine crease marks formed between his brows, making him look very serious. "I was wondering..."

His voice trailed off, tentative and unsure, two emotions Alex found difficult to associate with this assertive man. "Yes?" she prompted.

He rubbed his temple with a long finger. "I was wondering, would you like to have dinner with me tonight?"

His question registered, igniting a frenzy of elation. *Finally!* Not about to let this opportunity, or this man, slip through her grasp, she blurted, "I'd love to!"

He chuckled and tipped his head, regarding her with amusement. "Are you sure you don't need a little time to think about your answer?"

She shook her head adamantly. "No, I'm absolutely certain I'd love to spend the evening with you."

"Great. I'll pick you up at your room at seven."

Feeling giddy, she nearly floated as she headed toward the hotel, not to page Merrilee, but to make an afternoon appointment at the exclusive boutique for some sophisticated advice in purchasing a new, sexy wardrobe. While Jackson had a way of making her feel desirable, she wanted to look the part as well and didn't have the first clue how to accomplish that goal.

As she stepped into the air-conditioned lobby, it dawned on Alex that she hadn't given Jackson her room number. Then she laughed. If he was truly her fantasy man, she wouldn't need to.

4

"HERE YOU GO, Mr. Witt." Christy, the helpful sales-woman who'd spent the past hour assisting Jackson in selecting an array of women's apparel, opened the double doors leading to a spacious room in the back of the boutique. She waved him inside. "You can wait in our private dressing area for Ms. Baylor to arrive. I put the items you selected for her over there on that rack and table, and if you need anything else, just press this intercom on the wall and I'll come on the line."

"Thank you, Christy." Jackson had never been inside the intimate sanctuary of a woman's dressing room before and found the experience incredibly stimulating. He glanced around the room, reminiscent of a woman's boudoir, complete with a sitting area decorated in soft and soothing mauve and blue, and a large dais in the middle of the area. Floor-to-ceiling mirrors flanked the length of one wall, which reflected the entire room from different angles. Fresh-cut roses arranged in various crystal vases scented the air with a light, floral fragrance, adding to the alluring atmosphere.

The setup was perfect for what he had in mind.

He turned to the other woman with a satisfied

smile. "I'd like my presence to be a surprise for Ms. Baylor."

"Yes, sir," Christy said with a nod. "I'll send her in after she's selected a few outfits of her own."

Once Jackson was alone, he took a seat in one of the comfortable chairs upholstered in soft, luxurious suede to begin his short wait for Alexis. When he'd returned to his beach suite after his swim at the pool, there had been a voice mail message on his phone informing him of Alexis's afternoon appointment at Seductive Pleasures, a boutique on the island that catered to a woman's sensual side.

The moment he'd walked into the shop he'd been surrounded by silk and lace, eye-catching clothing and lingerie, and decadent feminine indulgences guaranteed to pamper a woman's body and soul...and stir a man's libido. He couldn't deny that touching wispy, delicate underthings and fingering slinky, sexy dresses and outfits, *and imagining them on Alexis,* had aroused every one of his five senses.

He intended to pamper Alexis's body and soul. He'd teased and flirted with her this afternoon, heightening the awareness between them and establishing that he wanted her. Now, he was going to tempt her and leave her craving *more.*

The sound of muffled female conversation drifted from the outer room, and though he couldn't make out what either of the women were saying, a quick glance at his watch confirmed that Alexis had most likely arrived for her appointment. After a few more minutes the door to the dressing room opened and Alexis stepped inside behind the saleslady. The other woman held a couple of outfits over her arm, and Alexis followed her across the opposite end of the room to the brass rack where Jackson's items hung. Neither woman glanced in his direction.

Christy slipped the hangers onto the end of the rod and smoothed out the dress, skirts and blouses Alexis had selected. "If you need anything else, just let me know."

Alexis drew a deep breath and released it slowly. "I'm sure these outfits are just the beginning of my transformation from plain and practical to sexy and enticing."

A secretive smile curved Christy's mouth. "I'm certain they are."

Alexis cast her companion a puzzled glance, but made no comment as she watched the saleslady leave the room, securing the door behind her. Once she was gone, Alexis turned back to the rack, stepped closer, and bypassed the clothing she'd chosen for the wardrobe Jackson had favored. Her fingers fluttered over the apparel, perusing each item with interest. Though Jackson couldn't see her expression, he didn't miss the way she suddenly stiffened, as if realizing she was intruding on someone else's selection.

Snatching her hand back, she stepped toward the white slatted door where a customer could change in private before viewing her appearance on the dais. "Hello?" she called tentatively. "Is someone else using this changing room?"

"No," Jackson replied from across the room. "Those outfits are for you."

With a startled gasp she spun around, causing her braid to swirl over her shoulder and slap against her chest. Her pleasure at seeing him was unmistakable, her smile genuine with a hint of sensual delight. Then the elation lighting her pretty eyes was quickly replaced with confusion.

"Jackson," she said, her voice husky and breathless—a provocative combination that sent a rush of heat straight to Jackson's lap. "What are you doing here?"

He shifted in his seat and reined in his unruly hormones. For now. "You requested assistance in selecting a new wardrobe for your stay here on Seductive Fantasy, and I'm more than happy to oblige."

He watched her swallow as she considered that. "How did you know I'd be here?"

"If a man desires something bad enough, he'll find a way to get what he wants. By any means possible."

His statement held a double meaning for Jackson, but there was only one connotation for Alexis to grasp. *And I want you.* The unspoken, but undeniable words dangled between them—tempting, teasing, seducing...

She drew a shuddering breath, and he clearly witnessed in her crystal-clear blue eyes that she wasn't used to being the recipient of such a forward overture. That contradiction again—the ruthless businesswoman he'd conjured in his mind clashing with this uncertain woman standing before him.

"Why are you doing this?" she asked.

Her tone didn't hold an ounce of suspicion, but rather was laced with a hint of that damnable vulnerability that wreaked havoc with his personal plans for retribution, and made him question who and what she really was.

He gave his head a slight shake. This woman was capable of duping men, of duping *him*, and though he found himself undeniably attracted to her, he vowed his interest in her would remain purely physical, for the sake of *his* fantasy.

But his fantasy meant doing and saying things that would breach *her* emotional barriers, and he strove to say just the right thing to make her bend to his will.

Standing, he slowly closed the distance separating them and stopped inches away. "Why do I want to be a part of your 'transformation'?" he asked, repeating the same word she'd used with Christy minutes ago. At her nod for him to continue, he discovered that the right words to sway her came much too easily to him, too honestly. "Because I want to make you feel desirable and beautiful, and what better way to do that than spending an enjoyable afternoon with you in a sensual boutique, watching you model different outfits for me?"

"You're going to *watch*?" Her eyes widened in stunned disbelief, and her voice squeaked.

He chuckled as modesty, and shock, colored her cheeks a fascinating shade of pink. "Well, you do have a private changing room, but I'd like to see the outfits on you, especially since I picked them out." He blinked lazily and grinned. "I also thought you might like a man's perspective of what's sexy."

Turning away from his speculative gaze, she focused her attention on the rack of clothing and viewed the various pieces he'd selected. All were tasteful in design, yet underscored with sensuality in some way. She stopped at a culotte outfit in chocolate brown and beige, and worried on her lower lip. While conservative compared to some of the other choices in the boutique, she apparently had mixed feelings about the hem of the shorts, which ended inches above the knee.

She tossed an indecisive smile his way. "Well, I do have to admit, your taste and mine are very different."

"Maybe I just see you differently than you see yourself," he countered as she thumbed past that outfit and onto a teal patterned sarong-style skirt that would reveal a fair expanse of leg, as well. "Be a little daring and adventurous, Alexis."

Her gaze shot back to his, amusement dancing in their depths. "Have you been inside my head?"

Caution rippled through him. Had he slipped up somewhere and said something he shouldn't have? Something he couldn't have possibly known but had learned from Mike?

He kept his expression casual and composed. "Why do you ask that?"

"Because you seem to know exactly what I've been thinking since arriving on this island."

He shrugged, playing through previous conversations they'd had. "Didn't you say you were here to cram a lifetime of missed opportunities in one week?"

She tipped her head. "Yes, I guess I did."

"Well, here's your chance to do exactly that."

She stroked her hand down the front of a silky tank top in a vibrant shade of purple. "I guess when it comes right down to it, old habits die hard."

"This is the place to let go of any inhibitions and enjoy whatever comes your way."

Her chin lifted a fraction as her confidence blossomed. "You know, you're absolutely right."

"Of course I am," he drawled. Reaching out, he touched his fingers to her temple, where her flesh was warm, smooth and soft, making him curious to find out if her skin was equally alluring elsewhere. "And just for the record, Alexis, I *do* want to be inside your head. I want to know everything about you." And in the course of that exploration, he was determined to unearth the woman who'd used him and his company to gain her own success.

But for now, with her looking up at him with such undisguised wanting, he focused on leading her directly into temptation. With mesmerizing slowness, he caressed his fingers down her cheek, strummed them along her neck, over her collarbone, all the way to the tip of her braid resting just above her breast. He resisted the impulse to stroke his fingers over the crest, to feel her body's reaction to his touch. As it was, his own body was restless and aroused.

"I want to know what you desire," he went on, his voice a low, masculine rumble that reflected her potent effect on him. "I want to know who you are, what you like, and what feels good to you."

He felt a shiver course through her. She swayed toward him, her irises darkening with the beginning glow of passion. *"You* feel good to me," she whispered.

He tamped a raw groan of pleasure, wishing her moist lips weren't so close to his. Close enough to capture with his own mouth and taste the sweetness within. Wishing, too, that he didn't want her as badly as he did. In ways that defied reason and his quest for revenge.

"That's an excellent start." He took a much-needed step back and shoved his fingers into the front pockets of his jeans, effectively breaking the spell between them. "Now why don't you try on something that feels good against your *skin?"*

The corner of her mouth lifted into a sultry smile, and without saying a word, the wicked twinkle in her eyes said it all: *his touch felt good against her skin.*

His hands tightened into fists in his pockets to keep from showing her just how incredible his bare skin would feel against hers. "The clothes," he murmured, nodding toward the array of items awaiting her.

"Of course the clothes," she replied, seemingly enjoying her attempt at practicing her feminine wiles on him. She checked the tag hanging from one of the summer dresses he'd chosen and glanced back at him in surprise. "How did you know I wear a size twelve? You claim to have a great imagination, but do you have X-ray vision, too?"

He chuckled at her sassy tone, relieved that she was beginning to relax with him enough to tease, and eventually trust, him. "No, nothing so supernatural or exciting as that. When you made your appointment, you gave the saleslady your size. I'm nothing if not resourceful."

She draped a few articles of clothing over her arm. "And full of surprises."

He added a pale peach, satin and lace nightgown, along with a matching robe on top of her selection, wondering if she'd be bold and uninhibited enough to try on the set in front of him—which was his reason for giving her the lingerie in the first place. "All pleasant ones, I hope."

"So far, I have no complaints." She took in the sexy, semi-revealing garment he'd placed in her care, and there was no doubt in his mind that she understood his silent invitation.

Something stirred deep within him, a combination of desire and anticipation. He was anxious to see if Alexis accepted his challenge, one that would undeniably strip away her physical reserve...and allow him that much closer to her emotionally.

THE TRANSFORMATION had begun. While Alex recognized her dark, braided hair, light blue eyes and ordinary features, she wasn't familiar with the woman reflected in the mirror wearing a short summer dress unlike anything she'd ever worn in her entire life. But Alex couldn't deny that she liked the winsome feeling enveloping her...of finally emerging from the sensible and simple lifestyle she'd adapted to at a very young age and embracing something far more carefree and fun.

With an engaging smile on her lips that came much easier than she'd ever expected, Alex twirled in front of the mirror in her private changing room, loving the feel of the light, flowing material swirling around her legs and caressing her thighs. The dress was made of soft lemon crepe and ultrafeminine in design with antique cream lace lining the snug bodice and peeking out from the hem. The style flattered her curves and enhanced her full breasts and slender calves in a way she'd never before dared.

She was beginning to realize the sensuality inherent in a woman's body, *her body*, and how an outward change of appearance could make her feel desirable and incredibly tempting. It was an uplifting, thrilling experience, one she embraced wholeheartedly.

Having spent her adult years following in her uncle's footsteps learning the computer business because it interested her and cemented the bond between them, Alex had never taken the time to nurture her softer, sensual side. She'd never delved the depths of physical pleasures, had never experienced true passion, had never indulged in fun, exciting, heady sex. No man had ever encouraged her to explore that aspect of her femininity.

Until Jackson.

Now she understood what she'd missed all those years working late nights on the design for *Zantoid*, rather than dating. She didn't regret her sacrifice though, because her dedication to Gametek had paid off; the company was finally finding its foothold in the computer industry.

But this fantasy, this one uninhibited, glorious week of pleasure, was her chance to make a man want her, to make *Jackson* want her, no holds barred. He'd supply those sensual memories for her to store, as well as give her the one keepsake that would last her a lifetime.

The freedom to let go of the restrictions that had ruled her life and pull out all the stops to entice a man was intoxicating. That fresh sense of liberation followed her as she stepped out of the dressing room to model her first outfit for Jackson.

While he sat very casually in a chair across the room, his intense gaze tracked her progress up the three steps leading to the large dais in front of the mirrors. She caught his reflection and held his stare, her recently bolstered confidence wavering just a bit. The man was so damn gorgeous, so attentive, it was difficult for Alex to believe he was all *hers*.

She inhaled a deep breath to relax, felt her breasts strain the confines of the fitted bodice and watched as his eyes dipped to that full, rising cleavage. "I have to admit," she said, her voice slightly raspy, "I never would have picked out a dress like this for my-self."

He tipped his head, dragging his gaze upward again, searing her skin with his slow perusal. "It looks great on you." His voice was a deep, drugging timbre. "The dress is soft. Romantic. Feminine. Just like you."

A melting heat settled in her belly, and lower, causing the insides of her thighs to quiver in a strange, but pleasant sort of way. "Flattery will get you everywhere," she said, light and teasing.

"That's what I'm hoping." His reply was serious

and straightforward, while the lazy wink he gave her promised there were more compliments to come. "But what I said is the absolute truth. You're a very sensual woman, and the clothes you wear should reflect that."

She considered his generous comment as she took in her appearance, seeing herself through Jackson's eyes. In the dressing room she'd mentally convinced herself of her physical appeal, but as she scrutinized herself yet again she saw another stage of transformation. There *was* an aura of sensuality shimmering around her, a luminous glow that brushed her skin in a soft peach hue and brightened her eyes to a startling shade of blue.

She liked what she saw and used it to her advantage, sending a coquettish glance his way. "Well, I think it helps that you have exceptional taste."

He shrugged, a smile twitching his mouth. "I know what I like on a woman and you have a voluptuous figure meant to be displayed, not hidden."

She traced the thin strap holding up her dress, finding her exposed flesh sensitive to her own touch. "I'm working on it."

"Good." Bracing his arms on the sides of the chair, he steepled his fingers in front of him. "So why wouldn't you have chosen an outfit like this for yourself?"

Her first response was to tell him that it wasn't her style. While there was truth in that reply, it was more of a convenient excuse. Her hesitation had nothing to do with fashion, but rather not knowing just how good she'd feel wearing a dress that accentuated *so* much.

Something deep within her urged her to be open and honest with him, to divulge more. She didn't question the impulse. "I never considered wearing something that shows so much..."

"Skin?" he supplied, amusement threading his deep voice.

She laughed lightly. "Yes. After my parents died, I was raised by my bachelor uncle who didn't know how to cater to a girl's whimsical side. He opted for a practical approach in parenting, and that didn't include pretty dresses."

A fond smile touched her mouth. Despite her Uncle Martin's unconventional ways in raising her, there had never been any doubt in Alex's mind that he'd loved her. He'd done the best he could, taking on the unexpected responsibility of nurturing a child when he'd been a man who enjoyed his solitary existence. He'd made her a part of his life, which was centered around his computer business, and she'd learned to adapt.

She shifted her gaze back to Jackson and found him watching her intently. Absently, her fingers played with the antique lace tickling her bare thighs as she continued her explanation. "I wore jeans and T-shirts all through grammar and high school and grew up more a tomboy than a little girl who wore ruffles and frilly outfits."

And that sensible lifestyle had extended to other aspects of her childhood, too. Barbie dolls had been replaced with computer games and tea parties had been substituted with lunches and late-night dinners with her uncle at Gametek while he worked on his latest creations. And from there, she'd learned the trade and shared in her uncle's dream. There had never been any daily feminine influence in her life to explain the intricacies of wearing makeup and styling her hair, no one to introduce her to the subtleties of how to dress to attract a man's eye, or how to flirt and tantalize the male gender.

"Sounds like you've got a lot of *Seductive Pleasures* to make up for," Jackson said, cleverly tying in the name of the boutique to his comment.

Seductive Pleasures. Alex liked the sound of that, especially coming from Jackson. "It's all part of those missed opportunities I mentioned."

He agreed with a sexy smile. "Then let's move on to the next outfit and see where all this leads."

Her pulse leaped a notch. Another dare. The man was a master at issuing subtle challenges, and it was up to her to take the kind of personal, intimate risks she'd never allowed herself to take. She wasn't a gambler, but this ultimate payoff was one she couldn't refuse.

With a small turnabout that flared the hem of her dress and gave Jackson a peek of more smooth flesh, she sashayed her way back to the dressing room. Feeling his burning gaze on her backside, she smiled to herself, suddenly intent on shaking up his composure as he sat so nonchalantly in the chair across the room. She wanted a physical kind of reaction from him, and set out to get one.

As she tried on and modeled each successive outfit

he'd chosen for her, she grew bold in the privacy of the spacious dressing room. She flirted and teased Jackson in a way she'd never before attempted with a man. If his sinful grin and the darkening of his eyes was any indication, he appreciated her efforts, enjoyed them even. He encouraged her to be uninhibited, was lavish with his praise, and she basked in her newfound sensuality and grew more confident of her feminine appeal.

Other than shifting occasionally in his seat, Jackson remained in his chair...too far away and too much in control.

Feeling sexually restless and frustrated that Jackson wasn't equally so, Alex returned to her secluded changing room, deciding she needed to deliberate a new strategy to arouse Jackson to the point of shattering his restraint. She wanted, *needed*, tangible proof that he found her irresistible.

She flipped through the last half dozen outfits hanging from a brass hook on the back of the door, looking for just the right item to suit her purpose. Her search came to an end when she came across the silky nightgown and matching robe he'd given her. For the past hour she'd deliberately bypassed the sexy lingerie in lieu of *clothing*, but now realized this ultimate dare, issued by Jackson, was the perfect device to use against him and gain the leverage she sought.

Feeling a burst of anticipation, she quickly stripped off the purple tank top and capri pants she'd just tried on, setting them in the "purchase" pile. She slipped into the negligee, shivering as the satiny, pale peach material slithered over her body, from the thin straps over her shoulders, to the hem swirling around her ankles. Scalloped lace lined the bodice and molded to her breasts, hinting at her rosy nipples beneath the mesh. A slit in the gown showed a fair expanse of leg. She reached for the matching, shimmering robe and wrapped it around her, securing the front with the sash. Satisfied that the sensual ensemble would get a rise out of Jackson, she drew a deep breath and stepped back into the outer room and slowly, sultrily, made her way up to the center of the dais.

She looked at her provocative image in the mirror, and gradually shifted her gaze to Jackson's reflection. Though he remained sitting, there was no mistaking the surprise in his eyes, as well as other noticeable changes. Gone was the lazy, laid-back demeanor he'd adopted during her display of outfits. His bold, masculine features had grown taut with awareness, and his body seemingly radiated a primal, virile tension.

She couldn't contain the thrill of victory that coursed through her veins. "You didn't think I'd try it on, did you?"

"I wasn't sure," he admitted, his voice low and deep.

She wove the end of the wrapper's satin sash between her fingers, giving it a gentle tug that unraveled the loops of the bow, but kept the tie intact, tempting him.

Never would she have believed her own brazenness could excite her so much. "Do you like it?" she asked.

"What's not to like?" He consumed the length of her through heavy-lidded eyes, leaving her breathless and he hadn't even touched her. "But the important thing is, do *you* like it?"

"Yes." Wanting the distance between them gone, she upped the stakes. "I also like how you're looking at me."

"And how's that?" he murmured.

She wet her lips with her tongue. "With dark eyes. *Hungry* eyes. As if you'd devour me if you could."

He made a low, growling sound deep in his throat...a hungry sound that verified he indeed had a voracious sexual appetite and *could* eat her up. "You're teasing me."

Tipping her head, she grasped the end of her French braid and slipped off the elastic band. "So it's working then?" She summoned a beguiling smile as she slowly unraveled the woven strands, then combed out the soft tresses with her fingers until her thick hair layered over her shoulders in bountiful, raven waves. "I wasn't sure if I was having any effect on you, considering you haven't moved from your chair since I started trying on all the outfits you chose for me. This one included."

Abruptly he stood and climbed the steps to the dais. Startled by his sudden approach when he'd remained so passive for the past hour, she spun around to face him, wondering what he intended to do. She'd *finally* gotten a response out of him, and as her gaze caught sight of the impressive erection pressing against the fly of his jeans, she wondered if she'd pushed him too far.

Heart pounding and skin flushed with warmth, she jerked her eyes back up to his face. He looked so dark, so intense...so sinfully, devastatingly male. A bundle of raw, untamed energy that was focused solely on her. He stopped inches away and stared down at her. He was so tall, so big, she had to crane her neck back to meet his gaze.

A small frown marred his brows. "Problem is, you affect me too much."

He seemed truly bothered by that fact and she sought to reassure him. "Why is that a problem? Seems to me it could be a mutually beneficial situation."

Those same dark brows shot upward in surprise. "An affair?" he asked, clarifying her insinuation. "Is that what you want?"

An affair. Hot. Wild. Exciting. Everything she was feeling at the moment, and everything she wanted to pursue to the extreme. With him. She was divulging part of her fantasy, but figured she couldn't be any more obvious or blatant about wanting him than she'd already been, so being upfront and honest about what she longed for made little difference at this point. In fact, it was probably the best approach for her to take.

"Yes, an affair is what I want," she said, speaking half of her fantasy out loud. "What about you, Jackson?" *Is that your fantasy, too?*

He touched her unbound hair and rubbed a lock between his fingers, seemingly fascinated with the texture and the waves she rarely let loose. "Being with you is *exactly* what I want."

The breath Alex hadn't even realized she'd been holding until that moment whooshed out of her lungs. Just like that, their liaison was settled. No more doubts, uncertainties or second-guessing his intentions. This gorgeous, sexy man would be the one to give her the kind of pleasure and passion she'd only dreamed about. And, if all went as planned, he'd be the one to father the baby she yearned for. A child that would complete her life and fulfill that aching need to have the family she'd lost at too early an age.

But she couldn't help thinking that her wishes seemed like a one-sided proposition. "What are you getting out of this?"

He dragged his thumb along the curve of her jaw, down her neck, and followed the line of the robe's lapels to the sash tied loosely around her waist. "Five days with a woman who intrigues me, arouses me and makes me want to discover her deepest, most intimate secrets. I want to seduce your mind, your body, your soul."

"*Yes*," she breathed, wanting that, too.

He smiled with lazy satisfaction. With a pluck of a finger the slippery sash came undone and the front of her wrapper draped open, catching, just barely, on her breasts before revealing the gown beneath.

She swallowed, unable to concentrate on anything but her body's lush, sensitive response to his featherlight touch. Gently, he eased her back around so she faced the mirror once again, so she could observe her rapt expression and witness her own gaze turning a hazy, sensual shade of blue. He stood behind her, the length of him brushing her spine, her bottom, her thighs. Her toes curled into the plush cream carpeting as she waited to see what would happen next.

He dipped his head so his mouth was near her ear and his breath stirred her hair. "Open the robe for me, Alexis."

She shivered at his direct request, and without hesitation complied. With a shrug of her shoulders, the silky outer garment slipped down her arms and pooled on the floor around her feet, leaving her clad in the revealing nightgown.

She sucked in a startled breath as he settled his hands on the indentation of her waist and skimmed his palms upward to her rib cage. Incendiary heat speared through her, traveling from the tips of his fingers to her breasts, her belly and between her thighs. Her knees went weak, and when she swayed backward he provided a firm, muscled wall for her to lean against.

She placed her hands over his much larger ones, wishing she had the nerve to move them higher, over her straining, aching breasts. Her nipples were tight and hard and clearly defined beneath the lacy webbing of the bodice.

Closing her eyes to block out the erotic images reflecting back at her from the three mirrors on the wall, she grasped the fortitude to urge his touch higher. He obliged, cupping her breasts in his palms. He squeezed and kneaded the plump flesh, then caught her nipple between his thumb and fingers. She moaned in pure, unadulterated pleasure.

"Have you ever touched yourself?" he murmured against her ear.

Her pulse skipped an erratic beat. Despite his very personal question, she couldn't lie. "S-s-sure."

His thumbs grazed the stiff crests, and there was nothing she could do to stop the whimper of need that escaped her or the way her head fell back to rest on his shoulder, which thrust her breasts more fully into his hands.

"Intimately?" His voice was low and raspy, as if he was struggling against his own desires.

Her entire body trembled as provocative, forbidden images danced against her closed eyelids. "Y-y-yes," she admitted. But it had never, *ever* felt like this before...so exquisitely acute and deliciously exciting.

His mouth, open and damp, moved along her cheek to her arched throat. "While wearing something so soft and sensuous?" He nuzzled her neck, then tasted her skin with a soft, warm lap of his tongue.

Deep in her stomach, muscles coiled tight. She shook her head and barely managed a strangled, "No."

"Aah, a first for you, then." He easily switched the position of their hands, trapping her flattened palms beneath his yet keeping his fingers entwined with hers so he was still touching her, too. "Caress the satin, Alexis," he urged, sliding their laced hands lower. "Rub it against your skin, your belly, your thighs...."

She did all that, and more, following Jackson's lead with shameless ease. With her eyes closed, she grew bold and savored every new sensation. The fabric was cool beneath her palms, yet their dual caress seared her flesh. He made her touch and feel curves and softness, building the anticipation of something far more erotic. And as inhibitions peeled away and she explored with an abandon foreign to her, his breathing grew heavy and his burgeoning erection pressed insistently against her bottom, making her feel voluptuous and desirable...and giddy to discover that he so blatantly wanted her.

Skirting the edges of the forbidden, he dragged their still entwined hands down her thighs, then up again, slipping inside the slit in her gown. She gasped as she skimmed across bare, smooth skin, then moaned as her fingers, then his fingers, grazed the slick heat dampening her panties.

Her breath hitched in her throat as shock waves of pure, carnal bliss beckoned to her. Her knees buckled, and he caught her with a muscled arm secured around her waist. A harsh hiss of air escaped him, and he pressed their touch deeper, increasing the erotic pressure and arousing her to a fever pitch of need.

"Open your eyes, Alexis, and see the transformation."

At his urging, she lifted her lashes and barely recognized her metamorphosis, yet acknowledged that this sensual woman in the mirror was a result of Jackson's coaxing and ministrations. Dazed, she took in the cascade of hair framing her face, her slumberous, darkened eyes, the pouty lips that had yet to taste the pleasure of his kiss, and the body that was outlined in clingy satin and lace. Unable to help herself, she followed the disappearance of both of their hands and felt a renewed rush of silky, liquid warmth settle against their fingertips.

She bit her lower lip and met his gaze as he watched them, and she saw the restraint in his expression. "Jackson," she moaned, trembling, so incredibly close to the edge of what she believed would be the most incredible orgasm of her life. And she wanted to experience it with him. Here. Now.

He knew. His eyes blazed with the knowledge and something else she couldn't quite decipher. Satisfaction, maybe? Triumph?

Before she could analyze that last emotion further, he completely distracted her thoughts with one last luxurious caress that alluded to a deeper ecstasy as he slowly, gradually withdrew their touch from beneath her gown. Lifting her hand to his lips, he placed a kiss on the tips of her still damp fingers, then tasted the very heart of her with a flick of his tongue. The intimate gesture, his heated, ragged breath, the throb of her unfulfilled body, all combined to send her into sensory overload and heighten her desire to an excruciating level of wanting.

A need he didn't plan to appease. Not here. Not now.

"Tonight," was all he said, but the one word held a wealth of meaning and promise. He placed a chaste kiss on her temple, so at odds with all that they'd just shared, especially when she wanted a *real* kiss, then released her.

Without another word, he turned and exited the dressing room, leaving Alex standing alone on the dais and feeling as though the entire encounter with Jackson had been some kind of luscious dream.

Or a very seductive fantasy come to life.

5

AT PRECISELY five minutes to seven Jackson strode through the luxurious lobby of Seductive Fantasy's main hotel. Finding the elevator, he stepped inside and hit the third-floor button to Alexis's suite. Only then, when he was alone and the brass and mirrored cubicle was slowly climbing upward, did Jackson allow doubts about his own personal motives, his fantasy and his quest for revenge to filter through his mind.

All afternoon, since leaving Alexis at the boutique after their provocative encounter, he'd managed to avoid his conscience and all the complex questions clamoring inside his head. Questions he *still* had no answers to.

He'd worked out in the gym, swam dozens of laps in the pool, and attempted to relax in the sauna. Unfortunately, nothing had taken the edge off his desire for a woman who'd somehow, someway, gotten under his skin. A woman he had no business wanting for anything more than to even a score between them.

He rolled his shoulders beneath his linen sports jacket to shake off the uncertainties he didn't fully understand, and blamed only himself for his current state of frustration. He'd *never* meant for things to go so far between them today. Despite that her desire for an affair made his fantasy easier to accomplish, seducing her mind and body through verbal tactics had been his only goal. Caressing her breasts, touching her intimately and stirring intense hungers he hadn't even known existed hadn't been on his agenda.

But as a woman who'd suddenly discovered her appeal and sexuality, she'd provoked him in the most breathtaking manner and he hadn't been able to resist the temptation she posed. Somewhere between lusting for revenge and skimming his fingers along her soft, smooth skin and watching her candid response to him, all his plans for retribution had vanished.

In one hour's time, she'd broken through the reserve and caution that had ruled the better part of his life where women were concerned. In the heat of the moment he'd crossed that fine, emotional line he'd drawn for himself and made her a tantalizing promise for tonight that would include more touching, more caresses. He'd make good on his promise, but wouldn't make love to her. And he vowed any trust and intimacy would be one-sided—*hers*.

It couldn't be any other way.

The elevator pinged its arrival on the third floor, and as Jackson stepped out he shored up his immunity to Alexis Baylor and reminded himself of his intent. Seducing her mind and soul was his priority. Keeping his own emotions detached was a necessity.

With that lecture solidified in his head, and feeling once again in control of the situation, he knocked on the double white doors with the gold numbers 305. His resolve scattered seconds later when Alexis appeared in front of him—a gorgeous vision in a sinful red dress designed to capture a man's attention.

And capture his, it did—from the off-the-shoulder design of the sleeves and low scooped bodice, to the sinuous, slim-line fit of the crushed red velvet that accentuated her curves to just below her knee. Shimmering stockings encased her slender legs, and strappy red sandals added a few inches to her height. Hell, even her toenails were painted a head-turning shade of scarlet, which matched her freshly manicured fingernails.

Heat lapped through his veins, and he swallowed to replace some of the moisture in his mouth. "I'm looking for Alexis Baylor," he said, summoning a perplexed expression while scratching his temple in mock confusion. "Is she here?"

She grinned at his playful comment, but there was enough doubt shimmering in her gaze for him to realize that she'd gone to great lengths to be so adventurous and daring. "Come on, Jackson. Stop teasing." She tilted her head, causing glorious, shiny waves of ebony hair to cascade over her shoulder.

He noticed that it was a few inches shorter than it had been that afternoon, and that it had been layered to make the most of the thick, silky mass. A light application of makeup enhanced her features, bringing out flecks of gold in her eyes, and a sheen of crimson-hued gloss coated her lips. A light floral scent surrounded her.

Obviously, her "transformation" had included a

complete head to toe makeover that had produced
very captivating results. He'd seen the potential for a
striking beauty, and here she was in the flesh. And
she was all his for the taking.

She was looking at him expectantly, anxiously,
and he found it too easy to give her the compliment
she deserved. "You look *incredible*." Reaching out, he
skimmed a finger along the cuffed sleeve that exposed her shoulders, and slowly followed the neckline to the creamy soft swells of her breasts which
rose and fell with each of her deep breaths. "You're
also full of surprises," he murmured. "I don't recall
picking out this dress today, and I'd remember you
trying it on, which I most definitely do not."

She laughed, the sound a beguiling mixture of
nerves and delight. "You like it, then?"

He raised a dark brow as he gave her another slow
once-over. "'Like' is a tame description for a dress
that makes you look not only sexy as hell, but good
enough to eat." He tucked a finger beneath her chin,
keeping her gaze locked on his when she would
have glanced away, encouraging her to feel and ac-
knowledge the smoldering heat between them. "Just
like that ripe, juicy strawberry you had earlier today
by the pool."

She licked her bottom lip, as if remembering the
sweet taste of the fruit. "I tried the dress on after you
left the boutique today, along with a few other things
I hope you like." A sultry smile curved the corners of
her mouth.

Despite his attempts to remain physically immune
to Alexis, her newfound boldness—a bewitching

change he was partly responsible for—excited him in ways that defied his logic. And damn if she didn't make him feel good, too...deep inside, in places deprived of a woman's gentleness, understanding and unconditional acceptance of Jackson the man, not Jackson the wealthy entrepreneur.

Right now, all Alexis knew was the man, and her honest reaction to him, coupled with the unfeigned wanting in her eyes as she met his gaze, made him wish this whole fantasy concept was based more in reality.

With an imperceptible shake of his head, he refocused on the here and now and the seduction he was enjoying more than was wise. "After that very tempting comment, it'll be all your fault that I won't be able to behave and keep my hands to myself tonight." He dropped his hands to her waist and let his palms drift lightly over her hips. "I want to find out what, exactly, this dress is hiding."

She smoothed her slender fingers down the front of his shirt, a sassy, impudent light brightening her eyes. "Maybe I'll let you."

His hands tightened on her hips, and with gradual pressure he drew her closer, so their lower bodies brushed enticingly, just enough to tantalize and tease. "Just so you know right up front, I want things from you that you've never given another man." Another truth he refused to analyze. "I want to do things to you and with you that just might shock you."

"I *want* to be shocked," she said, moving her thighs restlessly against his.

He nearly groaned as a hot jolt of awareness settled low, adding to the same primitive desire still simmering from this afternoon's encounter. This was *his* game, and though she was allowed to play, he was struggling to maintain the upper hand. "You'll do whatever I want or ask?"

She nodded, causing her hair to sway with the movement and the light behind her to weave through the strands, beckoning him to bury his fingers in the silken mass. "Anything and everything," she promised huskily, and without reservation.

He stroked his flattened palms around to the slope of her bottom and caressed upward, bringing their thighs, hips and bellies into sizzling contact. "Anytime, anyplace?" He wanted to know how far she was willing to go with him, if she was willing to shed every inhibition at a whim.

She entwined her arms around his neck, crushing her breasts against his chest. Softness to hardness. Heartbeat to heartbeat. Her fingers slid into the hair at the nape of his neck, her thumbs gently massaging the taut muscles there. "Anytime, anyplace," she agreed in a husky whisper, then threw him an unexpected curveball of her own. "Will you do whatever I want or ask?"

Being at her mercy wasn't something he'd factored into his fantasy, but he wouldn't refuse a request of hers. "Absolutely, but I'm hoping that I'll be able to give you everything you want or need before you have to ask."

"So far, you've done a pretty darn good job of anticipating my needs." She blinked up at him, her smile irresistibly flirtatious. "What do I want now, Jackson?"

His gaze traveled over her pretty features, taking in the flush on her cheeks and the hazy blue hue of her irises. Her glistening lips were poised inches beneath his, tempting him to breach the scant distance between them to sample and taste his fill of her, and see where it all led.

His pulse ricocheted. How had he become so ensnared by her, so entangled in a web that *he'd* woven for the sole purpose of luring her? Had he become so lost in needs and desires that nothing mattered but pleasing this woman and giving them both exactly what they wanted? The only thing he could think of at the moment was what her guileless gaze was begging for, what his own body clamored for.

With one arm still banded around her waist to keep her flush against him, he feathered the tips of his fingers along her cheek and grazed his thumb beneath her chin. "Right now, this very minute, you want to be kissed."

"Oh, you're good," she breathed.

"It's what I want, too," he admitted, unable to stop the truthful response before it slipped from his lips. Lying and deceiving didn't come easily to him, no matter the circumstances. He'd always demanded honesty, in business and in his personal life, and he gave it in return.

He'd expected his attraction to Alexis to be fabricated, to be filled with lies and shameless tactics designed to persuade and entice her. What surprised the hell out of him, astounded him even, was that so far very little of his seduction, his coaxing words, was pretense at all.

Neither was the intense craving stirring within him. "Just so you know," he said, his voice low and raspy, "from here on out I don't plan to ask permission for what I want...."

Sliding his hand into the warmth and softness of her hair, he cupped the back of her head and brought her lush mouth to his, making good on his promise. The kiss should have been brusque and quick and detached, more a statement of possession than a quest for satisfaction. But Jackson had never been one to rush one of life's greatest sensuous pleasures when he had a warm, willing and eager woman in his arms. And Alexis was all that, and more.

So he took his time, taking things deliberately slow and easy. Her lips were slick from the gloss, and as he alternately nibbled and suckled on the soft, supple flesh of her lower lip he discovered that she tasted like ripe, juicy cherries. Damn, but she was sweet. He savored the flavor, and luxuriated in just how well she matched his lazy, thorough exploration.

Her hands slipped to his jaw and her lips parted in invitation, a silent plea he understood and answered. In gradual, tormenting degrees, he deepened the kiss until finally his tongue touched the velvet heat of hers, tangling softly, wetly, erotically. Intimately. He hardened in a flash, way too effortlessly and with entirely too much anticipation.

She clung to him and moaned, a sexy little purr of a sound that vibrated in her throat and radiated outward. She moved sensuously against him in a rhythm that matched the thrust of his tongue. Every curve of her body seared him, making his blood boil and his heart beat double-time in his chest. Drugging pleasure followed, pouring through his limbs like molten lava, intensifying his senses and dulling his mind to everything but the soft, generous woman in his embrace.

A woman who was entirely too open and honest in her needs, her wants, her desires. Her passion for him. Her trust was exactly what he'd been aiming for, but he hadn't counted on his own reaction to kissing her, or the urge to possess her so completely. Nothing about this moment was feigned for either one of them, and the knowledge nearly drove him over the edge of sanity.

He needed distance before he did something incredibly stupid...like guide her inside her suite, kick the door shut behind them, and sate his hunger for her in the most basic, elemental way possible. No matter how much he'd come to crave Alexis physically in such a short span of time, making love to her wasn't part of his fantasy or plan.

With more reluctance than he could ever have imagined, he dragged his mouth from hers, placed his hands back on her hips, and drew a deep breath to regain his composure. "If we don't stop now, we'll never make it to dinner."

She stared up at him with eyes heavy-lidded with arousal. "Ummm." A dreamy sigh escaped her, and she smiled at him in awe. "That was... *Wow.* I sure hope there's more where that came from."

He chuckled, fascinated by her genuine wonder. "First, we need to eat."

Before he succumbed to the temptation to give her more, he allowed her time to grab the red shawl and hand purse on the couch in the living room, then ushered her down to the lobby. He held her hand securely in his, and she fairly floated beside him as they made their way out the main doors of the hotel to the awning where the motorized cart he'd requested awaited them.

He helped her into the passenger seat, slid behind the wheel, and started down the wide pathway that led to other parts of the resort. He'd discovered that there were three restaurants on Seductive Fantasy, one in the main hotel, and two along the beach at separate ends of the island. In between were guest cottages with views of the shimmering blue ocean, solitary stretches of sandy-white beaches you could reserve for the day, designated sites that catered to numerous fun activities and other indulgences to accommodate the resort's guests.

Despite the gourmet menu and dancing each of the restaurants offered, tonight Jackson opted for a private tryst with Alexis, and a breathtaking view of the sun setting over the horizon.

Another few minutes, and he brought the vehicle to a stop in front of his cottage. Alexis glanced at him curiously. Her hair was slightly mussed from the pleasant breeze during their drive, and her cheeks still glowed with desire.

"Where are we?" she asked, resettling her shawl over her bare shoulders.

He set the brake and turned toward her, resting his wrist over the steering wheel. "We're at my cottage."

A frown puckered her brows. "I thought..." Her voice trailed off in confusion.

"You thought what?" he prompted gently.

"I guess I'm just surprised, which is a good thing since I love surprises, and you seem to supply them with ease," she said, smiling impishly. "I assumed we'd be having dinner at one of the restaurants on the island."

"I never said *where* we'd eat." He brushed a stray strand of hair off her cheek, finding it a good excuse to touch her and let his fingers linger on her smooth skin. "I thought we'd have a romantic, intimate dinner for two here at my place. Are you okay with that?"

"More than okay," she said, wrinkling her nose at him, "just so long as you don't expect me to do the cooking."

He slipped from the cart and came around to her side. Offering his hand, he assisted her out of the vehicle. "What, you don't cook?"

She sighed. "I'm embarrassed to admit it, but my cooking skills are somewhat lacking." She tucked her hand into the crook of his arm and followed him up the cobblestone walkway to the cottage. "My uncle lived on fast food because it was quick and easy, and on the rare occasion when he did decide to whip something up in the kitchen, it was strictly meat-and-potatoes fare. I learned to cook the basics by experimenting, but something tells me you wouldn't be satisfied with a can of soup and a grilled cheese sandwich."

"No, it would take *two* grilled cheese sandwiches to satisfy me," he teased, and enjoyed the sound of her light, infectious laughter wrapping around them. He opened the front door and gestured her inside. "And rest assured, I don't expect you to cook for me tonight, and you won't even have to help clean up the mess, either."

She cast him an upswept glance as she passed him into the small living room. "No? This date is sounding better and better by the moment."

He gently grasped her arm and guided her toward the adjoining dining room and kitchenette. "We have our own private waiter to take care of all that," he said, then introduced the man dressed in black pants and a starched white shirt, who stood beside a sideboard laden with various covered dishes. "This is Geoffrey, and he'll be serving us dinner and dessert."

The other man nodded formally and smiled. "Good evening, Ms. Baylor. Have a seat, and I'll pour the champagne." Geoffrey waved a hand toward the glass slider leading to the terrace and a table set with fine linen, crystal and silver. Three votives flickered with candlelight in preparation for nightfall, and the seductive vanilla scent drifting on the air and the soft music playing from hidden speakers added to the romantic ambiance.

Alexis stepped outside, set her shawl and purse on a nearby lounge chair, and walked up to the terrace's white wooden railing. "Wow," she breathed as her gaze skimmed the expanse of white sand, and an ocean such a deep shade of blue it almost hurt her eyes to look at it. "What a breathtaking view!"

"Yeah, the view is fabulous," he agreed as his gaze encompassed Alexis's curvaceous backside and slender legs, instead of the island's scenery. He came up beside her and smiled at the elation wreathing her face. "Another half hour, and we'll be able to watch the sun set. It's a gorgeous, not-to-be-missed sight."

Carefree laughter spilled from her lips. "I don't plan on going anywhere."

"That's good to know, because I'm not letting you out of my sight." He held out a chair for her and inclined his head for her to sit. "Not for a while at least."

Surprise and pleasure lit her eyes at his gentlemanly gesture, as if she wasn't used to being pampered and catered to. She settled onto the padded seat with a soft, murmured, "Thank you."

Jackson removed his sports jacket and draped it over the back of his chair before sitting in his own seat next to hers. Geoffrey appeared and withdrew the chilled bottle of champagne from a silver bucket of ice by the table. Popping the cork, he poured them each a glass, announced that dinner would be served in five minutes, and disappeared inside the house again.

Alexis curled her fingers around the delicate stem and lifted her fluted glass toward Jackson for a toast. "To each of our fantasies that brought us together," she said, a spontaneous note of joy infusing her voice.

Why his belly twisted with guilt in that moment, he couldn't rightly pinpoint. Maybe it was how she looked at him with such conviction and adoration, as if she truly believed he was a man who'd make every one of her wishes come true. Or maybe it was the fact that he wanted her to be just as *she* presented—an honest woman who desired him without exception or ulterior motives.

At this moment, for the next few days at least, that was exactly the kind of woman Alexis was. And damn if he didn't want to pretend for that short span of time that a woman, that Alexis, could accept him for Jackson the man.

Pushing the tangle of emotions aside that questioned every one of his reasons for being there at Seductive Fantasy, for being here with *Alexis*, he inhaled a deep breath and raised his own glass. "To *us*," he countered, and clinked his crystal flute to hers.

She took a drink of the bubbly liquid, then another, then set her glass on the table. She leaned back in her chair, a whimsical smile on her lips and her unfocused gaze lingering on something out toward the ocean. He watched, amused, as she slowly lifted her hand and touched her lips with fingers tipped in provocative red.

Reclining comfortably, he clasped his hands over his belly. "Are you okay?" he asked after a few seconds had passed with her still in a trance-like state.

Her gaze shifted back to him, the depths a soft, alluring shade of blue. "I'm great, actually. Can you believe I'm still enjoying the aftereffects of our incredible kiss? I feel as though I've had one too many glasses of champagne and I've only had two sips."

Jackson found it difficult to believe that he had the power to spellbind a woman so thoroughly with a mere kiss, though it certainly was a flattering thought. "I find it hard to believe that you've never been kissed like that before."

"Believe it." She ducked her head as if suddenly self-conscious and fiddled with her silverware. "Then again, I don't have a whole lot of experience in the kissing department to compare our kiss to."

A horrifying thought occurred to Jackson, something he'd never before considered because the notion never would have meshed with the original image of Alexis Baylor he'd conjured in his mind. Before he'd met her and discovered so many contradictions to his original vision.

"You're not a..." His voice trailed off. Christ, he couldn't even speak the words!

Her luminous eyes grew wide as she realized what he was trying to ask. "A virgin?" she supplied. At his still mute state, she laughed and shook her head. "No, not in the real, physical sense of the word. I've had sex, but you're making me realize just how much I've missed, and that quite possibly I've never *made love* before."

Jackson felt as though he'd swallowed a huge wad of gum that had jammed in his throat. He couldn't speak, didn't know what to say to her statement, a statement that had knocked him off-kilter. She was putting a whole lot of stock in him, and while gaining her trust had been a goal of his two days ago, and still was, he'd never expected her acquiescence to be so easy. Nor had he anticipated wanting to make love to her in return.

Luckily, the waiter arrived with their dinner and placed the china plates in front of each of them, filled with a generous portion of lobster tail, rice pilaf and buttered green beans. The interruption gave Jackson a few extra seconds to regain his equilibrium.

Once everything was delivered, Geoffrey set a small brass bell on the table between them. "If you need anything else, just ring for me." Then he was gone, affording the two of them complete privacy.

Curious about her past relationships, and wanting to discover more than what Mike had revealed in his reports, Jackson asked, "Have you had many boyfriends?"

She shrugged as she cut a piece of her lobster and dipped it into the drawn butter on her plate. "A few." Slipping the succulent piece of meat into her mouth, she sighed at the delicious flavor, and her tongue darted out to lick a smear of butter from her bottom lip.

Jackson's stomach clenched with awareness, and he glanced down at his own meal and pushed his fork through his rice pilaf. "Anyone serious?"

"One relationship, in college," she said, taking a sip of her champagne. "But it didn't last very long. And after that, I poured my time into my studies, rather than men. Not that I had a line of them beating down my door. I was very plain and quiet, almost to the point of being invisible. And when I didn't have my nose buried in a textbook, I was busy working

part-time for my uncle at his computer company."
Before Jackson could latch onto that opening to question her about her uncle's business, she smiled fondly and added, "And then there's sweet, devoted Dennis."

Swallowing a bite of seasoned vegetables that all but melted in his mouth, he summoned an inquisitive expression. "Who's Dennis?"

"A good friend who'd like to be much more." She dabbed at the corners of her mouth with her napkin. "Actually, he works for me at my company. I inherited that computer business from my uncle when he died," she revealed. "And Dennis has been with the company for years and has always been there for me in some capacity or another."

"And you're not interested?"

"Unfortunately, no, not romantically," she said softly, and with a note of regret. "Don't get me wrong. He's a great guy. I really do adore him as a friend and he's a big part of my life. And he has wonderful husband potential and will make the right woman very happy some day."

"But not you."

Finished with her meal, she set her knife and fork on the edge of her plate. "Silly as it may sound, and maybe as unrealistic as it may seem, I want what my parents had."

Jackson thought about his own parents, and all he could recall were sad memories of losing a wonderful, affectionate father who'd died when Jackson had been only eight, and bitter recollections of a selfish mother who'd spent her time trying to find another man to take care of her financially, while leaving him to fend for himself. At age sixteen, when he'd taken on his first part-time job at an electronics company, his mother had relinquished all responsibility to him, abandoning him for her latest millionaire quest...only to seek him out years later when her string of rich lovers had come to an end and she discovered just how wealthy her son had become.

Done with his own dinner, Jackson pushed his plate aside, right along with those disturbing and too vivid memories that threatened to drag him down to a place he had no desire to revisit. Not here. Not now.

"What did your parents share that you want for yourself?" he asked, genuinely wanting to believe that marriage could be different and wonderful for some people. Based on love, respect and that all-elusive trust.

Her gaze touched on the glorious sunset dipping below the horizon in spectacular shades of red, oranges and streaks of violet. The glow of the sun tinted her smooth skin, making it shimmer like the color of a ripe peach. "From what I can remember, my parents were head over heels in love with one another. Their affection was tangible. I never felt left out of their relationship, but rather a huge part of their love. That's something I've kept close to my heart since their death."

She glanced back at him, the melancholy in her voice matching the emotion in her eyes. "I'm sure that their kind of marriage and relationship exists for a chosen few who are lucky enough to have fate bring them together, but so far, I haven't been so fortunate. And I don't want to settle for less than a love that is pure, and a relationship that is based on mutual respect and trust."

A tall order in his estimation. What Alexis desired was so unlike the ruthless businesswoman he believed her to be. How could she blatantly steal something from someone and still want and demand respect and trust in a relationship? The two didn't go hand in hand, and added more layers of confusion to his thinking.

Alexis watched the last of the sun disappear over the horizon and continued. "I've spent the past four years devoting all my time and energy to keeping my uncle's company from falling into bankruptcy, and haven't really had any time to date a string of men, or allow myself to get swept up into a romantic relationship."

She sounded very pragmatic, but Jackson saw through the sensible speech to her heart's true desire. It was very apparent to him that finding a man who would court her and sweep her off her feet was exactly what she yearned for. "And so you're here, on Seductive Fantasy, to discover what you've missed."

She nodded and glanced from the darkness that had settled over the island, to him. The candlelight on the table flickered, tipping the ends of her wavy, ebony hair with golden highlights. "Yeah, that's part of my reason for being here," she said quietly.

There was more, and he couldn't deny that she'd intrigued and tempted him with that dangling bit of information. "And the other reason why you're here?"

Her hands settled on her lap, and she laced her fingers together over her stomach. "Is personal and private," she replied gently. Then a bemused smile curved her mouth, and her eyes danced with sass. "Unless you care to share your reasons for being here first?" she invited.

He chuckled, recalling how he'd said those same exact words to her on the plane ride over when she'd asked about *his* fantasy. "Touché," he murmured, giving her credit where credit was due. They both still had hidden agendas, and while it was obvious that they were each other's fantasies in some capacity, neither one of them were willing to reveal more than they already had.

Their waiter reappeared from the dim lighting inside the cottage to clear their dinner dishes and serve them each a slice of the rich, decadent dessert Jackson had specially requested to accompany tonight's dinner.

While Geoffrey topped off their glasses of champagne, Alexis took her first bite of the dessert. Her eyes rounded in amazement and sheer delight. "Oh, my God, Jackson. This is *wonderful*."

Her reaction was exactly what he'd hoped for. "I'm glad you like it," he said as Geoffrey stepped behind them to light the three torches along the terrace railing, which added just the right amount of illumination to their dining area. "It's Amaretto Crême Brulée, and the chef assured me that it would be pure bliss for the taste buds."

She hummed her agreement and took another bite, closing her eyes to savor the exotic flavor. "I love the taste of Amaretto," she said, slowly opening her eyes. "How did you know?"

Shrugging nonchalantly, he picked up his spoon and dipped into his dessert. "Lucky guess?"

Her gaze narrowed, but her expression remained playful. "It's that psychic ability of yours, isn't it?"

"I'm not admitting to anything," he teased. Especially not where and how he'd discovered that bit of personal information.

Once their waiter was finished setting the mood with the lighted torches, Jackson thanked Geoffrey for his services and dismissed him for the evening, which left him and Alexis completely alone. For the next few minutes he watched her indulge in the rich, Amaretto-flavored dessert. She devoured every last creamy spoonful and even had no qualms about finishing the last half of his brulée that he pushed her way.

Once she was done, she took a drink of her champagne and settled back in her chair with a contented sigh, looking well fed. At least one appetite was satisfied. He'd take care of more sensual cravings later.

She tipped her head and smiled at him lazily. "So, what about you, Jackson?" she asked, her voice low and husky.

He frowned, not having the first clue as to what she was referring to. "What about me?"

"Well, I just gave you my history with men and relationships," she said, studying him with languid curiosity. "How come some woman hasn't dragged you to the altar yet?"

His entire body tensed, and he forced himself to relax, telling himself she wasn't asking for anything more than reciprocal information about him. He knew he could have waylaid her question by deferring to the tried and true excuse that this was his fantasy and he didn't care to mix in reality. But in this aspect of his life, he had nothing to hide from her.

"Well, I'm definitely *not* a virgin," he said, taking the humorous approach.

She laughed. "That thought *never* crossed my mind."

Twirling the stem of his empty glass between his fingers, he stretched his long legs out under the table. "I guess it's the same old cliché that everyone uses. I haven't found the right woman yet."

"Are you looking?"

"No." The word escaped him, harsher than he'd intended. He gentled his tone and went on. "I was engaged a few years ago, and I'm not anxious to repeat the process any time soon."

A frown touched her brows, and the flame from the torches flickered in her dark eyes. "What happened?"

He rubbed a hand over his jaw and inhaled a deep breath. "I thought I knew her, I most certainly trusted her, and I found out a few weeks before the wedding that it wasn't me she wanted, but what my money could buy." Too late, he realized just how much he'd disclosed, but a part of him didn't regret revealing something that had burned like acid in his gut for the past four years. In fact, it felt damn good to finally let some of the bitterness out into the open.

She didn't seem at all bothered by the resentment that had crept into his voice. "And so now..." she prompted, obviously wanting him to share more about his experience and how his ex-fiancée deceiving him had affected his view on relationships.

With more candidness than he thought possible with Alexis, he shared some very personal information. "And so now, I find it hard to trust women and their motives."

"Jackson..." Her voice reached out to him in the shadowed darkness, soft with compassion. "Not all women are like your ex."

He guarded himself against her gentle logic, but somehow, someway, her tenderness and understanding found its way through his barriers. "No," he said, agreeing with her observation, but then he added his own rebuttal. "But in my experience, most women want something from me, so I've learned to be extremely cautious."

She looked visibly startled by his frank statement, and he immediately wondered if he'd managed to strike Alexis at the very heart of her conscience. Was she contemplating her own deceit with Extreme Software and how she'd used some faceless person for her own gain? Or was she thinking about the fact that she was using him now for her own personal fantasy, the part she wouldn't divulge earlier? And what would she do in this very moment if he revealed his true identity?

And why did he want to believe the best of Alexis when he knew the worst?

She scooted back her chair and walked up to the railing, staring out at the darkness of the beach and ocean. He gave her a few moments alone, because he needed the reprieve, too. His emotions were all a jumble; he was feeling things he had no business feeling—doubts, tenderness, and too much of a connection. He never should have opened up and shared any part of his past with her, but she'd coaxed the words from him with incredible ease.

He shored his crumbling defenses. Time to put the evening and his fantasy back into perspective. And that meant focusing his concentration on seducing Alexis.

6

ALEX CLOSED her eyes and breathed in the scents of the sand and ocean, and the warmth of the fire from the torches lining the terrace. A gentle, sultry breeze blew, trailing across her skin like a lover's caress. What she wanted, what she craved, was Jackson's touch. And she seriously doubted that he'd want to have anything to do with her if he knew her ulterior motive. Just like the other women in his life, Alex wanted something from Jackson, though not his money.

She wanted his baby. A child of her own created in the heat of a passionate affair she'd forever cherish and remember. A child of her own that would finally give her the sense of family and belonging that she'd struggled to find for most of her life. A child that would love her unconditionally and be the center of her life.

Her fingers clutched the wooden railing. She'd never expected to experience guilt and confusion over her decision to book this fantasy and conceive a child. Then again, she'd never expected to fall so quickly and so deeply for the man she wanted to father her baby—a man who made her feel special and beautiful. Not only was Jackson gorgeous, sexy and in his prime physically, but he possessed traits which she admired and which struck an emotional chord in her. She'd seen glimpses of honesty and integrity during the past two days, and learned through their conversation that he valued those traits.

He'd also made it clear that he didn't like being *used*.

As difficult as she found the task to be, Alex pushed her uncertainties aside and tried to soothe her conscience. They were both on this island resort by their own free will. There were undisclosed risks for all parties who decided to partake in a fantasy, considering everyone's requests remained personal and private unless the people involved decided otherwise. It was the nature of the fantasy element. All guests were aware of the gambles involved, and she and Jackson were still hiding their true intentions from one another, so, in essence, they were using each other.

Risks. There were a dozen of them. She was taking a chance on Jackson, by being with him and choosing him as the man to teach her all about desire and passion. In return, he was taking risks with his own fantasy, and with her, too. They both would walk away at the end of this week with their fantasies fulfilled, and without guilt or regrets from either party. It could be no other way.

She heard the creak of his chair and his hushed steps as he approached her from behind. Immediate awareness raced through her bloodstream, and her lashes fluttered open again, but she didn't turn around. He braced his hands on the railing next to hers, trapping her within his embrace while the heat of him brushed the length of her. The crash of the waves on the shore echoed the anticipation quivering through Alexis's body, and in that moment, any last lingering doubts she might have harbored about her fantasy disintegrated into dust.

No matter how selfish, she wanted this time with Jackson, along with everything he had to offer. For so many years she'd given—to her uncle, his company and her employees. Now this was her time to take and enjoy.

He lowered his head next to hers and rubbed his cheek against her hair. Then he whispered in her ear, "Are you ready for me to make good on my promise from the boutique?"

Her breath hitched in her chest as forbidden images invaded her mind, tantalizing thoughts so blatantly erotic her legs grew weak. "What promise was that?"

"The promise of pleasure." He trailed his fingertips lightly up her arms and across her bare shoulders, leaving goose bumps in the wake of his provocative touch. "And if I remember correctly, you made a few promises of your own earlier."

She swallowed to ease the tightness gathering in her throat...the same constricting feeling banding her chest and causing her breasts to swell against the bodice of her dress with excruciating sensitivity. "I...I did?"

"Uh-huh," he replied, the low, rumbling sound of his voice coursing through her with as much electricity as a live wire. His large hands leisurely stroked down her back in a silky caress, skimmed the outline of her waist, hips and thighs, then coasted around to the front and stopped on her belly. He splayed his long fingers there, branding her through the velvet of her dress, then slowly guided her back the inches separating them, until her bottom nestled against his hips.

She gasped and dug her nails into the wooden railing. There was no mistaking the erection straining the front of his trousers, and there was certainly no stopping the liquid heat that flowed through her veins and gathered between her trembling thighs.

He glided his lips teasingly along her jaw, making her ache to feel his mouth on hers and his tongue entwining seductively with hers. "You made a promise about letting me find out what you've got on beneath this dress."

Shivering at the pure male confidence infusing his voice, she reached up and touched her fingers to his lightly stubbled cheek and turned her head. She met his gaze, which glowed with a heat so intense she felt seared from head to toe and everywhere in between. With effort, she summoned a sultry smile. "I said *maybe.*"

His lashes fell to half-mast, and a sinful grin turned up the corners of his mouth. "I'll accept that challenge, Ms. Baylor."

"That's exactly what I was hoping for." She knew it wouldn't take much to persuade her to do his bidding, but she couldn't deny that she was eager to see what his method of coaxing might entail.

His flattened palms moved over the layer of velvet

covering her curves, creating an exciting friction everywhere he stroked. Through the material of her dress he set out to outline each piece of lingerie she wore, discovering with a sense of feel rather than sight. His fingers shaped to her breasts and dipped just inside the neckline to feel the texture of her bra.

"Pretty and lacy, not that I'm surprised," he said, his voice laced with husky satisfaction. "I'm guessing the color is black."

Her nipples peaked and her back arched in hopes of nudging his fingers just a few inches lower to the throbbing tips, but he deliberately withdrew his touch.

She groaned in frustration and wrapped her fingers around the railing again for much needed support. "After that tease, you'll have to find out for yourself."

He chuckled softly, and his warm breath, scented with the arousing flavor of Amaretto, stirred the loose hair against her cheek. "Don't doubt that I will. In time."

And he was in no hurry at all, tempting her mercilessly, making her restless with his leisurely exploration. He smoothed his hands down her midriff to her pelvis, causing her hips to instinctively jerk forward, yet he ignored her silent plea and continued his downward, spiraling journey. His knees dipped a little lower to allow his hands to slip farther down to the hem of her dress, then he straightened, slowly dragging his palms back up her thighs while the material of her gown gathered around his wrists.

Her skin simmered then caught fire. Her head

spun dizzily and her breathing grew ragged in anticipation of where those skillful hands were headed—
straight toward the very heart of her that had been
awaiting his touch since that afternoon. He discovered the exact kind of thigh-high stockings she wore
and didn't stop there, caressing his thumbs along the
soft skin of her inner thigh on his quest to her panties. He grazed the dampness that told of her desire,
then traced the triangle of material covering her
mound, across her thighs and up the line on each
side of her hips to her waist, bunching the hem of her
dress just as high.

Jackson remained intimately close, the cotton
blend of his trousers scratching enticingly at the exposed skin at the back of her thighs. "Stockings with
lacy, elastic bands, and silky panties trimmed in soft
lace," he murmured near her ear, accurately describ-
ing her undergarments. "Black, too, I'm betting."

Beyond goading him this time, all she could manage was a soft moan.

He edged his thumbs beneath the waistband of the
panties encircling her hips, and she bit her bottom lip
as he inched them down, stopping just as the lacy
band reached the slope of her bottom. From behind
her, his breathing sounded as labored as hers.

"I want them off, Alexis." His voice emerged low
and rough with restraint.

Refusing his request wasn't an option for her, not
after she'd come this far. "Yes," she whispered.

With excruciating slowness, with mesmerizing intimacy, he dragged the flimsy fabric down her
thighs, her legs, and finally let the panties drop to

pool around her sandaled feet. The hem of her dress fluttered back into place, but she still felt utterly exposed and naked.

"Step out of them, sweetheart," he said, and without hesitating she obeyed his gentle command.

Bending low, he scooped up the scrap of silk, then straightened again, stretching his arm out so that he was holding her panties in front of her. He rubbed the shiny material between his big, masculine fingers. "Black and lacy, just as I thought."

She laughed, the sound not nearly as light and carefree as she'd intended. "You win."

Leaning forward, he brushed his lips against her temple, the tender gesture so at odds with the need clamoring inside Alex. "I'd like to think you're going to win at this, too," he said, then stepped away.

What did he mean by that? And why did he leave her standing alone after arousing her to such a fever pitch of desire—hot, bothered and more turned on than she'd ever been in her entire life? Was he merely toying with her? Frustration nipped at her, mingling with other confusing emotions she couldn't firmly get a handle on at the moment.

Believing he planned to retreat inside the cottage, she spun around to stop him and found him moving her shawl and purse off the lounge chair. With a casualness that belied his own fully aroused state, he settled back into the upright seat, grinned playfully, and dangled her unmentionables from a finger.

A light breeze blew, rippling along the soft material of her dress, which in turn tickled her very bare bottom. She shivered at the alluring contact, liking the provocative sensation too much. Feeling a sexual charge, and wanting to see how far Jackson was willing to take this sexy game of his, she tipped her head toward him and regarded her undies with mild amusement. "So, what do I have to do to get my panties back?"

The torchlight cast intriguing shadows over his chiseled features, making him appear mysterious, irresistible and breathtakingly male. "I'm not sure that I'm going to give them back." He tucked the wispy panties into the front pocket of his slacks and patted the pocket for good measure. "I think they'll make a nice souvenir of our time together."

He was teasing her, possibly testing her. She wasn't about to let it end here, not when she ached for so much more. "And what do I get as a souvenir?"

He crooked a finger at her, his eyes glittering with wicked intent. "C'mere and I'll show you."

Unable to resist temptation, unable to resist *him*, she moved forward until she was standing next to the lounge chair. He reached out and touched his fingers to the back of her left knee, lightly caressing the ultrasensitive flesh there. She gasped as shock waves of pleasure coursed up her leg, adding to the tingling sensation that was gradually increasing in pressure and need.

He placed her knee next to his thigh on the lounge, then lifted his hand for her to take. A silent dare. She accepted, knowing without asking what he wanted her to do. With his help, she straddled his hard, mus-

cular thighs with her bottom resting against his
knees.

"Closer," he murmured.

Grasping her hips, he slowly dragged her forward, pushing her legs farther apart until her knees
bracketed his waist and the only thing separating
their aroused flesh was the soft fabric of his pants.
His bold move pushed her dress up around her
thighs, revealing the lacy bands of her stockings, yet
keeping her most private parts modestly hidden
from view, which made their position even more
erotic and sexy.

She dipped her head forward, causing her hair to
tumble over her shoulders and cascade around her
face. Her hands landed on his chest, and she was
somewhat gratified to discover that Jackson's heart
thundered just as frantically as her own. Their gazes
met, his eyes dark and his features etched with un-
bridled sensuality. That she had the ability to make a
man want her was a very exciting, powerful thing.
And in that moment, she felt wild, uninhibited and
completely shameless about satisfying their mutual
hunger.

She gulped much needed air into her lungs.
"Maybe this is something we ought to take inside."

He shook his head and skimmed his hands up her
spine, drawing her upper body nearer. "We're all
alone, Alexis. I made sure of it. Anything that happens out here will just be between you and me and
Mother Nature."

It was the only reassurance she needed. She didn't
stop him when his fingers grasped the sleeves of her

dress hugging her arms, and the bra strap beneath, and gradually pulled them lower, until the material caught around her elbows and he'd completely exposed her full, aching breasts to his hungry, reverent gaze. She felt a shudder pass through him, felt the rise and fall of his chest as he pulled oxygen into his lungs. Cupping her in his large hands, he kneaded the soft, waiting flesh and dragged his thumbs over the rosy, beaded crests.

Her head fell back, her back bowed, and a soft, mewling sound of pleasure escaped her. She felt him shift subtly beneath her, then he pressed his open mouth to her neck. His lips moved down her throat, trailing hot, moist kisses, searing her skin with his tongue and teeth and scattering her senses in a dozen different directions.

Needing to feel him, too, she fumbled with the buttons on his shirt, somehow managing to open them all the way to his stomach. She parted the material wide and slipped her hands inside to touch the muscle and sinew across his chest and down his torso. He didn't give her much time to explore as his head moved lower and lower, and his hands pushed her breasts upward, until a taut nipple brushed his lips and he was able to draw the hardened peak into his mouth.

Her lips parted, but no sound emerged. The deep suction of his mouth, the graze of his teeth, and the swirl of his hot, wet tongue teasing her nipple all combined to push her right to the cliff of an intense, all consuming orgasm...and he wasn't even touching her below the waist. She squeezed her thighs against his and whimpered.

He pulled away in that moment and stared up at her, seemingly stunned to realize just how fast and close she'd come to release with him only suckling her breasts. His breathing was hot and erratic and sexier than anything she ever could have imagined, but it was the sudden self-control she detected in his demeanor that prompted her to act quickly.

"No, no, no," she moaned in frustration, refusing to let this moment with Jackson, this much needed orgasm, slip away. She guided one of his hands down to her thigh in a silent invitation, framed his face between her unsteady palms, and pressed her mouth to his. "Please," she begged desperately, then coaxed his lips apart with her own and kissed him deeply, giving him no choice but to respond in kind.

The moment her tongue mated with his he groaned his surrender and gave her exactly what she craved. She gasped at his first probing, intimate caress against her slick folds of flesh, felt the velocity of a powerful release cresting like a wave within her. She was beyond wet, beyond ready, and when he pushed one long finger deep within her and slid his thumb over her swollen clitoris she flew apart, coming in a hard, fast rush of exquisite pleasure. She cried out without inhibition and rode the heights of rapture, swept beyond the realm of anything she ever could have imagined experiencing with a man.

Incredibly, the wondrous climb immediately began again, little tingles of awareness dancing across her still sensitive flesh despite the fact that Jackson had removed his hand from beneath her dress. Need poured through her, stronger than before, a want so explicit and urgent that it shocked her—and excited her beyond belief. She broke their kiss, tossed back her head, and slid against the thick erection straining the fly of his pants. Eyes heavy-lidded with passion, she rocked her hips in an instinctive rhythm, a slow back and forth motion as erotic as the actual act of making love.

He sucked in a sharp breath and gripped her waist to halt her seduction. "Alexis..." His voice vibrated with a warning, or a plea, she couldn't be sure. He clenched his jaw hard, his restraint nearly palpable.

Sitting astride him, she most definitely had the upper hand, and she made the most of her dominant position to entice him—with another shimmy of her hips, and the brush of her breasts across his chest. "*Please,*" she whispered. "Just one more time."

His eyes were dark and smoldering as he looked up at her, and choked laughter erupted from his throat. "Greedy wench. I don't think *I* can handle one more time."

"You're welcome to join me." And then she set out to tempt and tease him as he was so good at doing to her. She found the freedom to openly seduce him liberating, and used her entire body and every feminine wile she possessed to cajole him to the precipice...just to prove to herself that she could.

It didn't take long for his need to equal hers.

Swearing vividly, he clutched her hips, not to stop her this time but to guide her movements to match his slow, deep thrusts. She moaned at the keen ten-

sion spiraling tight in her belly, and lower. The force
of his erection grinding against her and the pulsing,
flaring heat between them propelled her to another
dimension...as it did him. His muscles contracted
and he bucked hard—once, twice, three times—and
let loose a low, guttural growl against her throat.

She heard the sound of her own passionate cries
and lost herself in yet another breathtaking, mindless orgasm that seemed to go on longer than the
first. Once her convulsions ebbed, she sagged
against Jackson, crushing her bare breasts against his
chest. She buried her face in the crook of his neck, her
limbs and muscles still quivering and humming with
the most luxurious vibrations.

He delved his fingers into her thick hair, gently
cupped the back of her head and held her close.
"Alex," he groaned, his breathing harsh, as if he'd
just finished running a marathon.

Yet beneath her his body was still rigid, while she
felt absolutely boneless and satiated. Confusion assailed Alex, making her wonder if she'd misjudged
his reaction. She could have sworn he'd come with
her....

Curious now, she lifted her head and saw the
strained lines bracketing his mouth and the fierce
frown creasing his brows. "Jackson, did you...?"

Jackson squeezed his eyes shut to block the image
of Alexis's radiant face as a flush of embarrassment—of all things!—crept up his neck and spread
across his cheeks. He couldn't believe that he'd actually succumbed to her persuasive tactics, but there
had been no stopping the raw, primitive emotional

and physical need that had raged through him with as much force as an unpredicted hurricane.

And that concerned him. Slaking physical desire based on mutual attraction and lust he could deal with. But surrendering to an honest-to-goodness emotionally gratifying release was not conducive to his goal to seek revenge on Alexis.

"Yeah, I did," he admitted gruffly, completely disgusted with himself and his lack of control with her. Somewhere along the way, the seducer had become the seduced, and that had been the last thing he'd expected. "I haven't done *that* since I was a teenager."

She glided her fingertips along his bottom lip, and smiled in a way that turned him inside out with wanting all over again. "I'm glad I wasn't alone that time."

Me, too, he almost said, but caught the profound words before they slipped out. The woman was tying him up in knots, making him forget that this was supposed to be a ruse, and not the real thing.

Yet she *was* real...flesh and blood, with soft skin, a sensual disposition and luminescent eyes that seemed to see to the very depths of his soul. He gave himself a hard mental shake, blaming the cloak of darkness and the intimacy of her curling into him so trustingly for his wayward thoughts, for wanting to believe this evening was more than just a fantasy. And damn if he didn't want to cling to the illusion that the woman in his arms was just as open and sweet and giving as she'd been moments ago. He was beginning to seriously wonder if she had a twin and he'd somehow ended up with the good sister rather than the evil one.

Yeah, right. To become complacent now would only serve to cloud his intentions and possibly ruin his plans. What he couldn't explain or find an answer for was why taking revenge against this woman was becoming a task complicated with so many uncertainties.

Scrambling to put emotional distance between himself, Alexis and his uneasy thoughts, he opted to lighten the mood. Finding the endurance to gather up a wry grin, he skimmed the back of his knuckles along her smooth jaw. "You certainly give an incredible lap dance."

Her smile widened, seemingly pleased with his compliment and herself. "You inspired me." Her playful expression gradually faded, replaced by something far more serious and intimate. Her gaze searched his in the shadows cast by the flickering torchlight behind her. "Jackson...I want to make love with you."

It took every ounce of discipline he possessed to remain outwardly calm when she'd just presented him with yet another obstacle he had to overcome. He never planned to make love to her, and realized while tonight had been an unexpected trip to pure bliss with her, he'd have to do some fancy avoiding and exert strict control over himself to make sure he didn't go so far again. His fantasy was about *her* seduction, not *his*, and he'd do well to remember that.

Yet the hint of vulnerability in her eyes made something shift within him. He didn't want to hurt her, or make her think he didn't want her. The crux of his problem was, he wanted her too damn much.

He ran a finger down the slope of her pert nose, keeping his tone gentle and kind. "Considering what you and I just did, I think making love now is out of the question." As for the rest of their time together, he'd figure out how to avoid this kind of predicament as the situation arose.

She laughed, causing her still naked breasts to quiver enticingly with the vibration of sound, distracting and tempting him. Drawing lazy patterns with her finger around his nipple, she cast him a coquettish glance. "I'm more than satisfied for tonight," she agreed huskily, "and so are you, but...I need to know..."

"You need to know what?" he prompted, surprised by her sudden hesitancy with him. Unable to look at her lush curves any longer without caressing them, which would no doubt lead to the kind of trouble he'd sworn to avoid, he arranged the sleeves of her dress back into place.

She pulled in a deep breath and exhaled slowly, as if needing extra fortitude to continue. "I had a complete physical before I came here to the resort, and I received a clean bill of health." She paused again, swallowed nervously, and went on. "When was the...um, last time you..."

"Had a physical?" he finished for her, finding her modesty way too endearing. At her nod, it struck him that not only was she cautious and discriminate, but he suspected she didn't do this kind of thing often. And that knowledge shouldn't have pleased him as much as it did. "Eight months ago," he told her, remembering back to the routine physical he'd taken. "Everything checked out fine, and I haven't been with anyone since then."

Relief filtered across her face before she relaxed against him, cuddling into his chest. "Perfect," she sighed.

Jackson's arms automatically slid around her. Yeah, the moment was perfect...much too perfect for his peace of mind.

WITH A LIGHTNESS in her step, Alex strolled through the lobby of the hotel after perusing the specialty shops and purchasing a few souvenirs for Dennis and friends back home. Certainly not the kind of souvenir Jackson had stolen from her last night and given her in return, but rather fun, frivolous gifts one would expect from a vacation.

Aah, last night, she thought, smiling at the erotic memories still so fresh and vivid in her mind. Her body still thrummed with pleasure, combining with the thrill of anticipation. Making love with Jackson. She couldn't have been more clear and honest in her desire for him and knew sharing that ultimate intimacy would be the single most provocative experience of her life. One she had every intention of enjoying to its fullest potential.

And Jackson had a whole lot of potential, indeed.

Glancing at her watch and noting that she still had another half hour to pass before meeting up with Jackson for the afternoon as they'd planned, Alex headed out the etched sliding glass doors leading to a lushly landscaped atrium. Hands clasped behind her back, she followed the cobblestone walkway in an easy stroll, enjoying the bright colors of tropical plants and the tranquil scenery, which included man-made waterfalls and a pond with Japanese koi.

She'd woken this morning at eight to a knock on her suite door. But instead of finding the man of her dreams, the concierge had greeted her with a gorgeous bouquet of exotic flowers and a note from Jackson to join him for breakfast in an hour at the outdoor restaurant overlooking the lush, meticulously landscaped golf course. She'd showered, changed into one of the new, comfortable short outfits she'd bought at the boutique, clipped her hair back to keep cool, and arrived just in time to watch him finish up at the eighteenth hole with a group of three other men. While he was into sports and working out in the gym, and she preferred reading and shopping, their individual interests didn't detract from their compatibility.

They'd eaten a hearty breakfast amidst casual conversation, easy laughter, and subtle, intimate reminders of what had transpired between them last night. Every look, every touch and caress only served to heighten the awareness simmering in her veins. Alex felt thoroughly romanced, pampered and spoiled by Jackson, and she wasn't ashamed to admit that she loved every bit of his attention. And even though she knew she was falling for him in a way that was involving her heart and emotions, she was all too aware that this was just a fantasy for both of them, and nothing permanent could come of their affair.

She'd just never expected that knowledge to make her wish otherwise.

She sighed and continued past a group of people enjoying brunch amongst the beauty and serenity of the atrium. Once she and Jackson had finished eating, he'd told her that he had a few things to take care of, and that he'd meet up with her later. That had been nearly two hours ago, and she was anxious to be with him again, to spend as much time as possible with him over the next few days.

A loud squawking sound jerked her from her thoughts and she glanced to her right and saw a bright, colorful parrot pacing back and forth on a perch in an attempt to get her attention. "Well, good morning to you, too," she said in greeting.

He bobbed his red and green feathered head. "Pretty lady! pretty lady!"

Enchanted by the bird, she stepped closer to the rock encrusted alcove. A shimmering curtain of crystal blue water tumbled from the fall behind the parrot, and the intoxicating fragrance of gardenias filled the misty air. "My, aren't you the charmer."

He squawked again and twitched his tail, preening for her. "Freddy want a cracker!"

She laughed and held her hands out, palms up. "Sorry, Freddy, I'm fresh out of crackers."

Seemingly miffed that she hadn't brought a treat, he turned away from her with a huff of his chest and muttered gibberish beneath his breath. Alex shook her head and grinned.

"That's exactly the type of look I love to see on my guests' faces."

Alex spun around, surprised to see Merrilee standing behind her when she'd thought she was alone. Merrilee seemed to be enjoying the lively exchange between her and the parrot with an attitude. "And what look is that?" Alex asked, tipping her head curiously.

Merrilee stepped forward to her side, an open, friendly smile in place. "The 'I'm having a wonderful time' kind of look. Actually, it's more of a glow, and I'd recognize it anywhere."

Alex *did* feel radiant and happy, from the inside out, and knew Jackson was solely responsible for her newfound confidence and the joy bubbling within her. "Well, I can't deny that I am having a wonderful time. And as for that glow...I suppose my fantasy has a whole lot to do with it."

An elegant brow arched Alex's way. "I take it everything is going well with Jackson?"

Alex nodded, not at all surprised that Merrilee knew she and Jackson were an item. It was Merrilee's job to be on top of everyone's request, as well as to make sure they were satisfied with the progress of their fantasy.

"You were right," Alex said, continuing along the cobblestone path with her hostess strolling beside her. "He's everything I asked for, and more."

"I'm glad to hear that." Merrilee cast her a speculative glance. "Are you still planning to try and fulfill the second part of your fantasy?"

Alex inhaled a deep breath, knowing exactly what

Merrilee was referring to. "Yes." She sat on a bench along the walkway with a view of the pond and the Japanese koi swimming there, and Merrilee followed suit. She met the other woman's gaze and saw understanding in the depths, and a hint of caution, too. "More than anything I want a baby, a child of my own."

More than anything... Even more than Jackson? a small voice in her mind asked. She wasn't one hundred percent certain of her answer. But the truth of the matter was, her fantasy didn't include Jackson, at least not in terms of forever. He was hers for the duration of her vacation, he had his own fantasy to fulfill, but there were no promises or talk of commitment between them, just mutual fantasies that had brought them together. For one week. Nothing more.

He lived his own life in Atlanta and she lived thousands of miles away in California. The distance separating them was a huge deterrent for any relationship. She had no idea what Jackson did for a living, but it was unrealistic to believe a part-time relationship would ever work in the long run.

She wanted that baby...and she wanted Jackson, too.

Her head spun with so many desires and needs she'd never anticipated. Yet all her issues boiled down to the same neat little package—enjoying her time here at Seductive Fantasy with Jackson, then returning to San Diego and reality, and leaving everything behind but the glorious, special memories she'd take with her. She'd settle back into her predictable, routined life, look forward to her impending motherhood, and deal with the allegations toward her company that awaited her.

Gametek's lawsuit. Alex's stomach lurched with the reminder. Being with Jackson made reality feel so far away, almost nonexistent, but someone was threatening her company, her livelihood, and she had a battle waiting for her back at home. One she intended to win. She wouldn't, couldn't, lose the company that had been so much a part of her life.

"You know, I never had any children with my husband," Merrilee said, bringing her back to the present.

Astonishment wove through Alex. "You didn't want kids?"

"Oh, I wanted them, very badly," she admitted with a wistful smile. "But my husband was impotent, and maybe in some ways it all worked out for the best."

Alex dipped the tips of her fingers in the pond, the cool water a wonderful contrast to the humid warmth of the day. "How so?"

"My husband was a very self-absorbed man and much older than I," she said, then went on to explain their relationship. "We married under extenuating circumstances after the true love of my life passed away. Oliver never would have given a child the time and attention he or she deserved."

Alex frowned. "But *you* would have loved that child." Just as she, herself, planned on making up for her baby's absent father. Her child would know more love than he or she knew what to do with. The kind of adoration and attention Alex had grown up wishing for.

"Without a doubt," Merrilee said emphatically. "And at first I did feel cheated that I was unable to have a baby, but as the years went on and my husband and I grew further apart, I became a firm believer that a child should have two parents to love them, if possible. A child is a gift to the two people who create it, and that joy and responsibility should be shared equally."

Alex knew Merrilee wasn't judging her or what she wanted, just offering her opinion on the matter and subtle, womanly advice from someone who'd once been where Alex was now. She respected Merrilee's comments, which gave Alex more issues to consider over the next couple of days.

"Hey, there you are."

The sound of Jackson's deep, sexy voice immediately filled Alex with a surge of excitement and elation, and they'd only spent a few hours apart. She glanced up as he approached, looking exceptionally gorgeous in a red polo shirt and navy shorts, his skin a shade browner from the time he'd spent in the sun that morning.

She popped up from the bench seat and took the two steps toward him to close the distance separating them. "How did you know where I was?"

He brushed his warm lips across her cheek, starting a conflagration of desire to stir in Alex's belly. "Haven't you learned by now—"

"That you have your ways?" she finished for him, and laughed.

He winked at her, a sinful grin curving the same mouth that had brought her so much pleasure the night before. "The concierge said you'd come out this way, and then the parrot back there kept on repeating 'pretty lady,' so I figured you couldn't be far."

"Freddy *is* quite a character," Merrilee said with amusement as she stood. She gazed at both of them standing together, appearing gratified by their flirtatious interaction. "Did Danielle get your special request taken care of to your satisfaction?" she asked Jackson.

"Yes, thank you." He wove his fingers between Alex's and gave her hand a tender squeeze. "Everything is set up just as I wanted."

"Wonderful." The pager on Merrilee's waistband beeped, and she glanced down to read the message display. "If you'll excuse me, I have another guest to attend to. You two have fun."

"We will," Alex said, and once Merrilee was gone she turned to the man beside her, giving him a chastising look. "What are you up to, Jackson?"

He feigned innocence. "Who? Me?"

She poked him in the chest. "Yes, *you.*"

His broad shoulders lifted in a nonchalant shrug. "It's another surprise," he told her. "This one for tomorrow."

She groaned in disappointment. "You're going to make me wait an entire day to find out what it is?"

"Aah, the anticipation," he teased, his eyes alight with mischief. "I guess we'll just have to keep you busy until then. There's a whole lot to do here at the resort. Croquet, lawn chess, walking on the beach, horseback riding, dinner, dancing...''

"Let's do it all," she suggested, feeling alive and energetic and not wanting him out of her sight again today. "Let's cram as much fun as we can in a day's time until we drop from exhaustion."

He thought about her idea for a moment, then grinned. "That certainly works for me."

7

"PACK AN OVERNIGHT BAG, a swimsuit and plenty of sunscreen," Jackson announced the following morning when he arrived at Alexis's suite to pick her up for another day together. He'd sent up a continental breakfast for her earlier while he'd worked out in the gym, along with another note, this one stating he had an adventurous afternoon in store for her.

"You're kidding, right?" she asked, her blue eyes wide with incredulity. Despite how late she'd gone to bed the night before, she looked refreshed, vibrant and eager to start the morning. "I mean, I can understand the swimsuit and sunscreen, considering we're surrounded by pools and the ocean, but where can we go on this island that's going to require me to pack an overnight bag?"

He waggled his brows at her. "I guess you'll just have to wait and see."

She propped her hands on her hips and narrowed her gaze, but a sassy smile twitched the corner of her mouth. "Has anyone ever told you that you're—"

He caught her around the waist before she could finish her sentence, stealing her breath and bringing her flush against his chest. The unexpected move caused the skirt of her pretty summer dress to swirl around their legs.

"Irresistible?" he supplied, his voice low and deep.

Her body relaxed against his, and her throaty laughter escaped on a rush of exhaled air. "I was thinking more along the lines of exasperating."

As if his hand had a mind of its own, his palm stroked down her spine and over her bottom in an intimate caress and she arched closer. Much too easily, his own body pulsed with instantaneous awareness and a deeper hunger that stirred his soul. "And you're extremely impatient."

"I haven't had many surprises in my life," she said, her voice soft with underlying appreciation as she fingered the collar of his shirt. "At least not positive ones. I'm beginning to think the anticipation of wondering what you've got in mind is going to kill me."

"I promise you'll love it."

She blinked up at him and flashed him a very sensual grin. "Well, I've loved all your surprises so far."

"Then trust me on this one, too."

"I do," she replied without giving her answer, or the unconditional trust she was offering him, a second thought.

The guilt that stabbed through Jackson wasn't anything he hadn't already experienced during this trip, just sharper and more intense than it had been before. It was getting more and more difficult to dismiss that nagging voice in his head that kept him all too aware that he was lying to Alexis. And worse, he was lying to Merrilee, too, all in order to further his quest for revenge.

Soothing his conscience with the fact that this was all a fantasy was beginning to wear thin, especially when the lines between fantasy and reality were beginning to blur. Settling a score with Alexis was his fantasy, and reality had yet to show him a self-centered, ruthless businesswoman capable of infiltrating another company to steal someone else's technology.

No, the woman he held in his arms was exactly the kind of woman he'd told Merrilee he wanted to meet, one he could open up to and trust. And that worried Jackson most of all because not only had Alexis effortlessly coaxed personal things from him he'd never intended to share with anyone, let alone *her*, he feared he could fall for her, too damn easily...if a part of him hadn't already gone and done just that.

She twined her arms around his neck and threaded her fingers through the hair at the nape of his neck, a slight pout on her lips. "So, how come you slipped out on me last night?"

"Me?" His brows raised high and he laughed. "You *literally* dropped from exhaustion." *And thank goodness for that*, he thought.

"I *was* tired," she admitted, her expression turning adorably sheepish. "But then again, we went non-stop yesterday."

And that request of hers to have as much fun as they could in a day's time had been his saving grace to keep their physical interaction to a minimum. Oh, they'd touched and kissed many times during the day, but they were never alone long enough at any one time to get entangled into an intimate, sexual predicament. After what had transpired at his cottage with his mindless surrender to Alexis's very sexy ministrations, Jackson was determined to keep the reins of control in his hands at all times.

So far, so good. His deliberate ploy had worked yesterday, but today was another day, and while he had a full afternoon and evening planned to keep them busy, he had no doubt it was going to be damn difficult to thwart Alexis's advances. She'd made it more than clear that she wanted to make love to him, and he had one ace up his sleeve to use that would keep him from getting involved with her sexually— and he was saving that hand for tonight when they were all alone and he knew she'd want to take their affair to its logical conclusion.

Making love to Alexis Baylor wouldn't, *couldn't*, happen, no matter how badly he was beginning to crave otherwise.

"You did say you wanted to 'do it all,'" he reminded her.

"True. And we had a blast, didn't we?" She smiled, as if remembering all the fun they'd had, all the laughter and playful moments they'd shared. The color that gradually infused her cheeks made her skin appear luminescent, the kind of glow that radiated warmth and happiness. "I think my final downfall was enjoying one too many piña coladas at the Players' Lounge last night."

"I think you're right." He rested his clasped hands at the base of her spine. "You were just a teensy-tiny bit tipsy by the time the band played their last song, and I've *never* taken advantage of a tipsy woman." Both issues were the truth, and he followed that up with a bit of teasing. "I brought you back to your room, put you into bed and you asked for a glass of water. When I came back from the kitchen you were deep asleep and snoring."

She stiffened and gasped in mock outrage. "I don't snore!"

He bit the inside of his cheek to keep from grinning. "How do you know?"

Her mouth opened, then snapped closed as she schooled her features into a very prim expression. "I'm *sure* I don't."

"If you say so," he said in a very placating tone of voice.

She looked appropriately miffed at his good-natured goading. "You really are exasperating."

"Irresistible," he refuted, whispering the word in her ear.

He felt a shiver ripple along the length of her body. "Yeah, that too," she murmured, going soft and pliant in his arms. She shifted against him with a sigh, sending a surge of pure lust skittering up his thighs and straight to his groin. The knowing smile tipping her mouth told him she'd felt the sexual electricity, too. "So, Mr. Irresistible, how about a good morning kiss since I didn't so much as get a peck on the cheek last night because of your very chivalrous nature?"

"I think I can manage to make up for that." He told himself he couldn't refuse without raising her suspicions, but even as he lowered his head and captured her lips with his own he knew he wanted this kiss just as much as she did—if not more, judging by the raw need she kindled within him.

The kiss started slow and sweet and quickly turned seductive and provocative. Lips parted and melded, tongues tangled silkily and delved deeply, and from there rapacious hunger took over. Her arms tightened around his neck, she rose up on tiptoe to get closer, and her breasts rubbed against his chest.

Cupping her bottom in his hands, he tilted her hips and slid a thigh between hers, pressing high, right where he knew she ached. Her breath caught and released on a moan that vibrated in her throat. Desire and arousal jolted through Jackson, searing his senses with fiery heat and uncontrollable urges. It was as though he couldn't get enough of Alexis— her honeyed taste, her feminine scent, the feel of her lush body molding to his, and the naked emotion in her kiss that devastated his defenses and shook the very core of his resolve to resist her. The sensual gyrations of her hips mimicked the slow thrust of his tongue, and his pulse quickened, warning him he was nearing the point of no return.

Control, control, control. It was slipping like a landslide and he shored every last bit of restraint he could grab hold of to end the kiss before he carried her off to the adjoining bedroom and gave Alexis exactly what she wanted…his body.

His soul.

The startling thought wove through his mind, snapping him out of the passion-induced fog ensnaring him. He pulled back and her lashes fluttered open and she gazed at him dreamily. Her face was flushed with pleasure, her lips wet and parted, and he gritted his teeth against the urge to dip his head and kiss her again. And again. And again.

Very gently, very reluctantly, he released her. "Go and pack that overnight bag before we get completely sidetracked and you never find out what my surprise is."

The mention of his surprise was enough to pique her interest and ward off an argument about just how satisfying being sidetracked could be. "I'll be right back," she said, and sashayed into the adjoining bedroom.

Jackson swiped a hand down his face and prowled around the living room in an attempt to shake off the restlessness pervading his body, as well as put his intentions with Alexis back into perspective. To seduce her. To secure *her* emotional involvement. And to walk away from this vacation with his own feelings intact.

A week ago his goals seemed so clear cut and easy, his plot for revenge straightforward and uncomplicated. But then again, he never believed he'd actually *like* being with Alexis, as well as enjoy their easy discussions and playful, sensual banter. And no way, no how, had he bargained on desiring her in very erotic, intimate ways that had nothing to do with retaliation, or even unadulterated lust. No, wanting Alexis was becoming an unexplainable *need* he was finding more and more difficult to ignore...a

dangerous need that was threatening every one of
his convictions and beliefs about Alexis, the woman.

Jackson paced past the end table next to the sofa
just as the phone there rang. With his mind on other
matters, he automatically picked up the receiver and
answered the call. "Hello?"

Silence greeted him on the other end of the line.

"Hello?" he tried again, his voice reflecting a hint
of impatience.

Very tentatively, a male voice responded. "Is this
Alex Baylor's room?"

That snapped Jackson back into the immediate
present and made him realize exactly where he was
and that he'd answered Alexis's phone. "Yes, this is
her room," he replied, curious to find out who the
masculine voice belonged to. Out of the corner of his
eye he saw Alexis walk out of the bedroom, her
packed overnight bag in hand. "Can I tell her who's
calling?"

"Dennis." His voice was cool, clipped, and not at
all thrilled to have to explain himself to another man
in Alexis's room.

"Just a second." Jackson held the receiver out to
Alexis. "It's Dennis."

Her eyes brightened with pleasure by several degrees as she tucked the phone against her ear. "Hey,
Merrick, how are things going?" She was quiet for a
moment as Dennis replied to her question, then she
glanced Jackson's way with a fond smile and a pretty
blush and said, "Oh, that was just a friend I met on
the island."

A *friend*. Jackson didn't even care to analyze why

the bland description of his relationship with Alexis caused a twinge of annoyance to ripple through him. Or why it made him want to touch her in ways that would make her reconsider her choice of words.

"Of course I miss you," she said sincerely as she twisted the phone cord around her finger. "This is the first time you and I have ever been apart this long."

Though Jackson knew she was just placating Dennis, he experienced an unwarranted twinge of jealousy right in the vicinity of his chest—a possessive spark he had no right or business feeling. But as he eavesdropped on her light, animated, comfortable conversation with the man who was interested in her as more than a business associate, the burning in his gut increased in heat. He inhaled a deep breath and forcibly dismissed his crazy thoughts.

Alexis rolled her eyes at Jackson as she continued to talk to Dennis. "It's only been a few days since I last called, Merrick," she said with a laugh. "This is supposed to be my vacation, and I didn't think I had to check in every day. I figured you had everything under control until I got back to the office and you'd call if something important came up." Her expression suddenly grew serious, and the coloring in her cheeks paled a shade, as if Dennis had just informed her that something important *had* cropped up in her absence.

"Just a minute," she murmured to Dennis, then covered the mouthpiece and met Jackson's gaze, her features etched with concern. "Give me a minute or two. It's business related."

She was asking for privacy, he knew. With a nod, he headed outside to the terrace, closing the screen door behind him, but leaving the glass slider open so he could still hear their conversation. He settled into one of the chairs so he could see Alexis at an angle, but pretended interest in the bright, colorful garden of plants and flowers below her suite.

"Go on," she said to Dennis as she lowered herself to the sofa. A few seconds later she gasped in shock. "Fred Hobson?" she asked incredulously, then absorbed whatever Dennis had to say with a frown. "Are the lawyers investigating the likelihood of that?" Another lengthy stretch of silence ensued, then she closed her eyes and pressed her fingertips to her forehead. "God, Dennis, I sure hope you're wrong about this. Just the thought of..." Her voice trailed off before she finished her sentence, and she shook her head in distress. "Well, the possibility makes me sick to my stomach."

The possibility of *what*, Jackson wondered in frustration as he tried to piece together Alexis's conversation with Dennis to decipher what, exactly, they were referring to. He recognized Fred Hobson's name as his ex-employee, who once worked for Alexis's company and was hired on at Gametek again after quitting Extreme Software. The same man he believed Alexis had sent to Extreme Software as a plant for the sole purpose of infiltrating the technology she'd needed for her new action-adventure game.

He kept an eye on Alexis and gauged her responses to her VP. What was bothering Jackson the most about this scenario was that she wasn't as worried as she should be when backed against the wall with a solid accusation that would incriminate her. She was more upset and disturbed by the situation than hostile, defensive or spiteful.

Jackson shifted uneasily in his chair as confusion assailed him. Her body language didn't convey culpability or guilt—and suddenly the strong, undeniable urge to confront Alexis with the whole entire situation rose within him. With effort, he squashed the impulse. Not only had he been privy to one side of a conversation that left him with too many unanswered questions, he wasn't prepared to enlighten her with his true identity just yet. Not until he figured out more about what was going on with her.

She pushed her fingers through her hair and sighed. "I know you're not trying to spoil my vacation, Dennis, and I can't tell you how much I appreciate you handling this while I'm gone." A facsimile of a smile softened her lips as she listened to her VP. "Okay, I will. But let me know if you or the lawyers come up with any solid information. I'll be in touch."

With a quiet, affectionate goodbye, she hung up the phone. She folded her hands in her lap and sat there on the sofa, looking completely dazed by whatever she'd discussed with Dennis. Jackson returned to the living room and she glanced up at him with a frown still creasing her brows.

"Is everything okay?" he asked.

"Things aren't so great back home." She paused for a moment, her gaze searching his, as if contemplating how much she wanted to share with him.

Then, seemingly deciding she could trust him, she said, "My software company is involved in a legal dispute that just got more complicated on my end of things." She shook her head and drew a deep breath. "Something unexpected was discovered about one of my employees when my lawyers started investigating the claim, and I'm more than a little stunned with the news Dennis dropped on me today. I'm hoping it's all a big misunderstanding or mistake."

Jackson pushed his fists deep into the pockets of his khaki shorts. "Want to talk about it?" A huge part of him—the part that wanted to believe that Alexis was as guileless as she presented herself— hoped she'd be the one to open up and confide in him about what had just transpired between her and Dennis on the phone and give him something, *anything*, to validate the frustrating doubts settling over him.

Much to his disappointment, she didn't.

"Actually, I'd like to forget about the problems awaiting me back home, because there isn't much I can do about any of it while I'm here." She stood, her somber disposition replaced with a burst of energy and revived determination. "I've got a swimsuit and sunscreen packed as ordered. I'm depending on you to keep me distracted and show me a good time, Jackson."

Knowing he couldn't pressure her into revealing something she wasn't ready or willing to share, he scooped up her overnight bag and focused instead on fulfilling her request. "I'll certainly do my best."

HE'D CHARTERED a boat for the two of them, a sleek, thirty-six foot cruiser named, appropriately, *Sea Sprite*, with accommodations and amenities as luxurious as the resort's suites. Alex was instantly delighted with Jackson's plans to spend the next day and a half sailing between and around the neighboring islands. They would do as they pleased, as the whim struck, whether it be basking in the sun, playing in the water, or taking the dinghy attached to the boat to the island to explore the beach and terrain.

Settling against the padded bench seat in the cockpit of the boat as they drifted along the calm sea, Alex pulled in a deep breath, inhaling the salty scent of the ocean. She lifted her face—which she'd slathered with plenty of sunscreen so her fair skin wouldn't burn—toward the early afternoon sun and watched as the sails above her billowed in the breeze. While Jackson had prepared to set sail earlier, she'd changed into a black one-piece swimsuit trimmed in gold, coated every exposed patch of flesh on her body with SPF-30 lotion, then tied a matching wrap around her hips and waist for fashion as much as coverage.

A contented sigh unraveled the last of the tension that had tightened her chest since Dennis's phone call. This relaxing cruise was exactly what Alex needed to put her recent worries and concerns aside for a while. Too soon she'd return to civilization and the problems plaguing her company. Too soon she'd have to deal with the possibility that a trusted employee of hers might have done the unthinkable and jeopardized Gametek's reputation—and could quite possibly destroy everything she'd worked so hard to build the past four years.

She refused to allow any of that to spoil her time with Jackson, and she trusted Dennis to take care of things and make sure their team of lawyers thoroughly investigated the new and startling information they'd unearthed on Fred Hobson. For the next few days she was going to clear her mind of everything but her intimate desires, and Jackson. The two went hand in hand, and if she had her way she'd be making love with Jackson very, very soon. He'd given her so much in their short time together, and that was one sensual memory she was determined to take with her when she left the magical resort behind.

She glanced up at the object of her thoughts, who stood at the wheel navigating the short course to the other side of Seductive Fantasy. He looked as comfortable and at ease as a seasoned sailor, and just as sexy and gorgeous, too, wearing just a pair of navy blue swimming trunks. The wind combed through his dark, silky hair, his broad, gloriously bare chest was a warm shade of brown from the kiss of the sun, and the grin he sent her way caused her belly to flutter and her heart to expand with effervescent emotions she was growing increasingly used to.

Yet despite his laid-back attitude, ever since they'd left her suite, since her call with Dennis, actually, he'd seemed preoccupied and distanced. She had no idea why, and sought to pull him out of his pensive mood.

"I don't know how you continually amaze me

with your ability to know exactly what will make me happy, but you did it again." She smiled at him and brushed back strands of hair from her cheek that had escaped the clip she'd secured at the nape of her neck. "So, tell me, how did you manage to get an incredible boat like this for us?"

"I'm coming to discover that anything is possible on Merrilee's islands," he said, his eyes scanning the far end of the island before meeting her gaze with a slight squint to ward off the sun's direct rays. "I asked her about chartering a boat for the day, and her assistant, Danielle, contacted a place in St. Lucie that was willing to bring a boat out to the island. I thought it would be a nice little getaway."

"Uh-huh," she agreed, letting one leg slip from the opening in her wrap to dangle enticingly over the side of the seat. She was gratified to see that he'd noticed her deliberately seductive pose. "A getaway from our getaway, with lots of privacy out here on the ocean."

He winked at her. "That, too."

And she had every intention of taking advantage of their seclusion when the time was right. "You seem to know exactly what you're doing. I'm impressed with your sailing skills."

His long fingers played along the polished wheel. "I pretend real well."

Used to his teasing, knowing he was toying with her, she laughed. "Seriously, where did you learn to sail?"

A nonchalant shrug lifted his broad shoulders, but the gesture lacked the complete casualness she suspected he'd been striving for. "I have a smaller thirty-foot cruiser back home and take it out on the weekends. It's my escape when my life gets hectic or stressful."

Aah, a glimpse into his private life. For the sake of their individual fantasies, she'd respected his need for privacy, but she couldn't help but hope that he'd give her more than bits and pieces that never seemed to add up to anything substantial. Considering how little he'd divulged about himself in comparison to what she'd shared, she was willing to take any morsel he was willing to offer and see where it led.

"You have a hectic life?" she asked, prompting him for more details.

"Don't we all?" he replied, his tone much too cavalier for Alexis's liking.

She bit the inside of her cheek in frustration. So much for her efforts to draw him out. He'd answered her question with a question of his own that didn't even require her to respond. And did she even have the right to expect him to open up to her with personal information when sharing that kind of deep understanding of each other had nothing to do with the fantasy she'd requested? With an internal sigh, she let it go and instead resurrected fond recollections of her childhood to share with him.

"I haven't been on a boat since I was a little girl," she told him, and he tipped his head her way, listening attentively. "Actually, it's been since my parents died. They owned a boat, and we went sailing off the coast of San Diego most weekends. They loved to sail and fly, and just be outdoors." And now, as an adult, she understood the appeal of her parents' recreational choices. The fresh air, the wide open spaces, all combined to relax and free a person's mind. "I didn't realize how much I missed sailing until now."

His eyes were a dark, striking shade of blue, and undeniably curious. "What happened to the boat after your parents passed away?"

She'd succeeded in capturing his interest, and that was enough to satisfy her for now. "My uncle sold it. He wasn't into sailing, or any other kind of outdoor recreation." Amusement rippled through her when she recalled more memories. "The few times I remember him joining us on a cruise he spent most of the time looking green and hanging over the side of the boat."

Jackson's deep, rich chuckle drifted on the breeze. The bow of the boat hit a small swell, sending a spray of water up on deck, cooling them both. The moisture beaded on Jackson's chest and arms, glittering on his bare skin, then quickly dried up from the heat of the sun.

"Ever thought about getting another boat now that you're older?" he asked.

She hadn't until today, when it occurred to her just how tedious her life had been for so long, centered around her uncle and Gametek, rather than her own personal pleasures. "Maybe someday, when I have someone in my life who enjoys sailing as much as I do." *Someone like you*, she thought, even as she knew the thought was a futile one. Her time with Jackson was limited. She had no right wishing for more.

So, she might as well enjoy *now*, because as far as

fantasies went, it didn't get any better than Jackson
and the exquisite way he made her feel. Shading her
eyes with her hand, she glanced toward the island
and resolved to make every moment with him count.
Resolved, too, to give him as much as she planned to
take so they'd both return home with special memories—memories that would have to last her a lifetime.

8

ALEXIS LEANED more comfortably against Jackson's solid, warm chest and took a sip from the glass of wine they were sharing. They sat on the padded bench one step below the deck, relaxing after yet another fun, busy day together. Nightfall had descended and a full moon had risen high in the sky, backdropped by a blanket of black velvet generously sprinkled with bright, glittering stars. The boat rocked with a gentle, lulling rhythm that matched the soothing sound of the water lapping against the hull.

Her bottom was nestled between his spread thighs, her head rested on his shoulder, and one of his arms lay across her waist. The cozy, comfortable position was one longtime lovers would share, but Alex was all too aware that they'd yet to cross that threshold in their affair. If they had more time together, she honestly wouldn't have minded the slow seduction that kept her body in a constant state of arousal, or the intimacy that pulled on her heartstrings and made her yearn for more than one week with this man. But knowing that she and Jackson would part ways soon made her that much more eager to make love and experience the culmination of all the anticipation that had been building since the moment she'd first seen him on the plane.

She just didn't understand why Jackson was resisting the blatant sexual pull so evident between them.

Another day had slipped away from them much too quickly. They'd taken the dinghy and spent an afternoon on the far side of Seductive Fantasy, following trails and taking in the beauty of the island. They'd gone snorkeling along the reefs, horseback riding on the beach, explored rock-encrusted caves they'd discovered, and she'd even coaxed him into building a sand castle with her, which had ended in a playful "sandball" fight. Once she'd tagged him with three straight shots and gleefully declared herself the winner, Jackson had scooped her up in his arms and carried her out to the ocean to rinse the grit off their skin. He'd stroked his hands along her arms and legs until she was thoroughly cleaned and breathless with wanting, and she'd returned the favor, boldly caressing him until he'd finally declared a truce before they went too far on a public beach.

Dinner had been a casual event, seated outdoors in their swimsuits at a small, quaint café where they'd fed each other shrimp and other delicacies with their fingers. They'd returned to the boat just as the sun was setting and he'd climbed up on the deck and offered her his hand to help her on board. She'd accepted his assistance, and experiencing a sudden burst of playfulness, she'd pushed him back overboard...but not before he'd caught her around the waist and brought her splashing into the ocean with him.

They'd laughed and frolicked in the water. She'd dunked him, he'd come up sputtering, and before he had a chance to return the deed, she'd wrapped her arms around his neck and kissed him—a hot, deep, wet kiss that quickly flared out of control and threatened to drown them both. A kiss that clearly said she wanted him. A kiss he responded to with just as much hunger.

Yet once they were back on the boat, he'd put distance between them again. He'd handed her a towel while he'd dried himself off and slipped a T-shirt over his head. Then he'd disappeared below deck and returned a few minutes later with a bottle of wine and one glass for them to share.

And now here they were, cuddling close with their swimsuits still on, yet the emotional distance he'd seemed to stake between them bothered Alex.

She decided it was up to her to breach those barriers once and for all. Sliding her hand along his arm, she intertwined their fingers together over her stomach. "You know," she began in a sassy drawl, "I'm beginning to think you're deliberately trying to exhaust me again today, just like you did yesterday."

Behind her, she felt the subtle stiffening of his muscles. "I just want to make sure you're having a good time." His voice was deep and even next to her ear. "And if I remember correctly, you gave me orders earlier to make sure I kept you distracted today."

So she had. He was a man who took orders seriously. What would he do if she issued a request that he make love to her? The sexy thought tempted and intrigued her.

"Well, I'm having a wonderful time, and I can think of many other pleasurable distractions we've yet to try." Tipping her face to the side so their lips were only scant inches away, she reached up with her free hand, slid her fingers into his still damp hair, and brought his mouth to hers. The kiss was slow and sweet, and tempered with too much reserve on his end.

With a barely suppressed sigh that reflected too much of her disappointment, she ended the kiss. He picked up the glass of wine he'd set on the deck and took a drink, then gave it to her to take a sip. The flavorful liquid tantalized her taste buds and settled warmly in her belly, but did nothing to take the edge off the desire he so effortlessly kindled.

She gazed up at the night sky and smiled to herself when she found the Big Dipper. "There were times when my parents took the boat out in the evenings without me, and now I understand why. It's very romantic floating out here on the ocean, all alone except the sea and the sky."

"They sound like they were very much in love," he replied, his voice low.

"Yeah, I think they were." She'd told him as much that night at dinner, but there was something in his voice that told her that he didn't fully believe such devotion could exist.

Before they ended up launching into a conversation that once again centered around her, she turned in his arms and looked up at him. The light filtering up from the companionway illuminated his features, revealing the reticence in his eyes. "You know, it seems like I'm the one always talking about me."

"I've told you things about me," he replied, his voice underscored with a slightly defensive note.

"A few," she agreed, smoothing her hand over his chest and wishing he wasn't wearing a T-shirt so she could touch his bare skin. "Tell me a childhood memory, Jackson. Something that really stands out in your mind."

He frowned at her. "Like what?"

She tamped down the swell of familiar exasperation rising within her. "Like...*anything*."

His gaze shifted away from hers, his reluctance to divulge any part of his past nearly tangible.

Deciding to change tactics, she shifted against him so that her legs entangled with his and she settled more comfortably against his side. Her face was nearly level with his, and his arm was still wrapped loosely around her back and waist. "Okay, how about I share a childhood memory with you, something I've never told anyone else, but you have to promise to give something in return?" His eyes met hers again, dark and shadowed, and though he didn't verbally agree to her terms, she was going to hold him to the silent pact. "Know why I like the taste of Amaretto so much?"

A smile hitched up the corner of his mouth, lightening the moment between them. "I have no idea."

Her fingers played with the ends of his hair. "Well, when I was about seven, I found a box of chocolate candy in my father's desk drawer at home. They were Amaretto-flavored truffles, and I used to sneak one every day after school. My father never said a word about the missing candies, and when his supply ran low a refilled box would always appear. We never talked about me taking those chocolates. It was like our own private little secret."

The sentimental recollection caused a well of feeling to crowd her chest, infusing her voice with long-suppressed emotions. "When I found out that my parents died, the first thing I did was take the box of candies from my father's desk drawer and I hid it so no one could take it away. I saved those chocolates for as long as I could, taking small bites at a time until the box was finally empty. And when all the candies were gone and the box didn't magically refill with more truffles, it finally sank in that my parents weren't coming back. Ever."

She drew a deep, calming breath and managed a smile. "Now the taste of Amaretto is like a comfort food, and it always brings back those fond memories of my father."

He stroked his knuckles gently along her cheek, seemingly touched by her story. "I wish I had something like that to share."

"Surely there's something that stands out in your mind as memorable."

He said nothing. The rippling sound of the sea and the clang of the rigging caused by the sultry night breeze echoed through the silence that had descended between them.

Instead of letting another bout of frustration get

the best of her, she took the direction of their conversation into her own hands. "Do you have any brothers or sisters?"

"No." He paused for a moment, then added in a quiet tone, "Like you, I'm an only child."

The tiny glimpse was a start, a piece of Jackson that gave him more depth and made her feel closer to him, more connected. "Are your parents still alive?"

"My father died from a heart attack when I was a little kid." This time, his answer came without a lengthy hesitation. "He was a kind, caring man from what I remember."

She waited for more, but knew she'd have to pry every last bit of information from him. "And your mother?"

"Is around."

His comment was so flippant that at first Alex thought he was attempting to be funny...but quickly realized that there was no accompanying flicker of amusement in his eyes, just an unmistakable bitterness that startled her. Something had happened to him with his mother, something that had affected him on a deep emotional level.

Yet despite the change in his demeanor, she still felt very safe and unthreatened in his embrace. And that knowledge and security gave her the fortitude to pursue the topic. "Is your mother not a part of your life?"

A rough, caustic laugh escaped him. "Only when she needs something from me, which is usually money."

She pulled back slightly, appalled and shocked by his statement and the hardness that had crept into his voice. He used the separation to let her go and sit up on the bench seat, planting both feet firmly on the ground. She sat up next to him, and before she could formulate a response to his comment, he went on.

"When my father died we didn't have much money. We lived in a small house that we must have rented, because I remember my mother telling me that we couldn't live there anymore after my father died. So, she gave away my dog, who was like my best friend, and we packed up and moved into a one-bedroom apartment." He braced his arms on his thighs, his brow furrowed as he stared at some invisible spot between his feet. "At some point, my mother picked up a job as a secretary, and I remember coming home from school one day to find her and her boss fooling around in the bedroom. I sat in the living room and waited until they were done, and when the guy walked out he completely ignored me and left. When I got angry with her because my father hadn't been gone all that long, she told me that her boss was going to give her the money she needed to get her out of the 'hell hole' we were living in."

He pulled both hands down his face and released a harsh stream of breath. Alex ached for him and what he'd endured as a young boy, and she had the awful feeling there was more. Drawing her feet up onto the bench seat, she wrapped her arms around her legs, and forcibly resisted the urge to touch him and offer compassion. Now that he was talking, she didn't want to risk shattering this intimate moment of trust between them.

He rolled his shoulders and glanced out at the murky darkness of the night beyond their boat. "Her boss obviously didn't give her enough money, because we lived in that apartment for a good five years," he said, his words vibrating with resentment. "And the affair didn't last, either, but that didn't stop my mother from finding other lovers she could use to support her financially. She constantly left me alone at night while she went out to bars, looking for the next wealthy guy to take care of her."

His jaw clenched tight, causing the tendons along his neck to pulse with the force of his underlying anger. "I hated what my mother was doing, hated that I was a second thought to the men she openly chased. I remember lying in bed at night waiting for her to come home, and during those dark, lonely hours I formulated a plan. *I* wanted to take care of her and be the one she depended on, and so that summer I took on odd jobs around the neighborhood, cleaning pools and mowing lawns for a few bucks, and digging through dumpsters for aluminum cans to cash in at the recycling place. I managed to save up almost two hundred dollars that summer, and being young and naive I thought that would be enough for my mother to get us a nice house and everything else we needed. I thought I'd be some kind of hero for her."

Finally, he met Alex's gaze, and the anguish glittering in the depths of his eyes reached out to her in a way she couldn't help but respond to. "Know what she did with that money?" he asked.

She shook her head, her heart already wrenching with pain for whatever he was about to tell her.

A sardonic smile edged up the corner of his mouth. "She went out and bought a new dress, spent the evening out, and returned home past midnight with a guy who wasn't happy to discover the morning after that there was a kid in the house."

"Oh, Jackson..." She swallowed back the huge lump in her throat, unable to put her empathy into words. For as much as her uncle had lived in his own world, at least she'd grown up feeling secure. She could only imagine how awful it had been for Jackson.

"That was the first of many lessons I learned from my mother," he said, seemingly not done with his tale. "When I turned sixteen and found an after-school job at an electronics company, my mother decided that I could support myself while she chased after some rich guy down to Louisiana. She left me on my own and would go months without contacting me, and when she did call it was to tell me how sorry she was for leaving me and being such a bad mother, and, of course, to ask for money. And like a fool, I gave it to her, hoping this time would be different, but it never was. She only wanted me for one thing, and still does. My money and what it can buy her. All I've ever wanted in return was her love and acceptance, instead of being used and taken advantage of."

A taut muscle in his cheek ticked, his eyes dark

and intense and brimming with raw emotion. "And every time I try to let go of the past, and begin to trust something or someone, I get suckered in again. Between my mother and my ex-fiancée, you'd think I'd learn."

He didn't *learn*, because he was a good, honest man who wanted to believe the best in a person, and that was an admirable, valued trait in Alex's opinion. Despite his outward strength and carefree attitude, Jackson was so very vulnerable inside. The pain she witnessed in his expression gave credence to the deep emotional wounds he harbored, and made her ache for him and everything he'd gone through.

"Those are the kind of memories I have, Alexis, from childhood to the present," he said, his voice low and rough. "They aren't very pleasant ones, are they?"

She couldn't deny the truth, no matter how she wished otherwise. "No, they aren't," she whispered.

He stared at her for the longest moment. An eternity, it seemed. Moonlight reflected off his masculine features, highlighting an odd combination of anger, frustration and need. It was the latter emotion she understood the best, because she felt it, too.

Then he shook his head, hard, and abruptly stood, as if realizing all that he'd revealed. "I'm going below to take a shower," he said gruffly, then disappeared down the companionway.

Alex hugged her legs closer to her chest and rested her chin on her knees, wondering if what Jackson had just shared with her had anything to do with *his* fantasy. To be appreciated for the man he was, and not what he owned. It made sense, considering his past with women. Yet she didn't know for sure, and had no right to ask or pry. She could only speculate.

She chewed on her lower lip, debating what to do—let Jackson go, or follow him down below. Making a split second decision, Alex stood up and followed the soft glow of light illuminating from the galley. This time she wasn't going to let him avoid her. There was only one thought filling her mind, her heart...and that was replacing Jackson's painful memories with pleasurable ones. Then he, too, would have something to take with him when they left the island.

AFTER HASTILY shedding his shirt and swim trunks, Jackson stepped into the small cubicle of a shower, a true luxury on a boat. Bracing his flattened hands against the resin wall, he dipped his head beneath the spray and let the lukewarm water rinse the salt and sea from his hair and skin. He grunted irritably, wishing the massage jets hitting his shoulders and back could wash away his doubts, confusion, and the startling need gripping him just as easily.

No such luck.

He had no idea what he'd been thinking, pouring out his darkest secrets and turbulent past to Alexis—a woman he'd sworn to keep his emotional distance from—when he'd never shared that part of himself with anyone. But she had offered him honest understanding, silent compassion, and the kind of acceptance he'd always craved. Her interest had been genuine, which made him all the more aware that he was deceiving her and keeping a huge, devastating secret from her. A secret that was slowly but gradually eating away at his conscience.

With a deep growl that seemed torn from his soul, he reached for the shampoo bottle, poured a dollop into his palm, and scrubbed it through his hair. When had everything become so complicated and mixed up? What he'd originally suspected and believed about Alexis Baylor had slowly diluted over the past few days, making him feel things for this woman that he had no business feeling. He was falling for Alexis, with his heart and emotions hanging on by a tenuous thread.

His mind replayed the time he'd spent with Alexis. He couldn't ever remember when he'd had such a good time with a woman, without any expectations attached. He hadn't even had to pretend that he enjoyed her company! Too easily, she made him forget his purpose for being on this trip, yet when he reminded himself of his reasons, so many uncertainties clouded his normally solid judgment. And after overhearing her disconcerting conversation with Dennis about Fred Hobson, Jackson was inclined to believe that there was more to this twisted tale of piracy than even Alexis realized.

But he didn't know for certain, and that bothered him most of all.

He rinsed his hair and worked on lathering up his body with liquid soap, wondering what the hell he was going to do about Alexis, his fantasy, and the undeniable attraction between them. Maybe they ought to return to the island tonight instead of spending the rest of the evening dodging temptation. Solitude would hopefully enable him to sort out everything in his mind and give him the opportunity to contact Mike and ask him to dig up information on Fred Hobson. He needed answers, and solid proof of Alexis's innocence.

Even as the notion filtered through his mind, Jackson already knew in his heart that he believed Alexis wasn't as culpable as he'd originally thought. Gut instinct prompted him to trust in his feelings, to trust in Alexis. That realization struck fear in him because he'd been in this situation before— giving trust, only to receive betrayal in return.

Finished with his shower and resigned to heading back to Seductive Fantasy, he reached to shut off the water just as the plastic curtain enclosing him in the shower opened. His belly tightened, as did other parts of his anatomy, as his gaze took in the sight of Alexis standing there, completely, beautifully naked. But what struck him most was that she seemed to be exposing herself emotionally as well as physically. While her body was stripped bare, revealing supple, feminine curves and smooth, pale skin, an unmistakable hint of vulnerability and wanting shone in her eyes—along with a silent plea that wreaked havoc with his determination to resist her. Blood roared from his head straight to his groin and settled there with sharp, almost painful intensity. He gritted his teeth. It didn't help matters that a pleased and very seductive smile curved her lips as she watched him turn impossibly hard and thick.

Boldly, wordlessly, she stepped into the cubicle

that was really meant for only one, crowding him against the far wall and leaving him no easy escape. She was so close his throbbing shaft grazed her silky thigh, sending another rush of sizzling awareness zinging through his veins. Then she moved under the showerhead. Closing her eyes, she tilted her head back and lifted her arms to her unbound hair. He watched, mesmerized, as the spray drenched her hair, sluiced over her face, then hit her shoulders and drizzled over her full, tight breasts, her rigid nipples, and rolled in intriguing rivulets down her belly, until her whole body was wet and slick and so very enticing.

His breathing accelerated to a harsh, aroused rhythm. She was making it extremely difficult for him to keep his hands to himself—and he was fairly certain that was her intent.

Her lashes slowly drifted back open, revealing eyes a gorgeous, honest shade of blue. She flattened her hand against his chest—right over his thundering heart—and leisurely dragged her palm down his torso and over his taut abdomen until she'd shamelessly encircled her fingers around his fierce erection. It took every ounce of strength he possessed not to buck against her snug hold on him.

She licked her bottom lip with her tongue, lapping up moisture from the shower. "Mind if I join you?" she asked huskily, sassily, just as her hand stroked upward and squeezed the sensitive tip of his straining shaft in her grip.

He almost came right then and there.

With a low curse, he grasped her wrist to stop her

sensual assault, but the words he needed to speak to end this delicious torment eluded him.

"Don't tell me no, Jackson," she said, as if reading his mind and sensing his hesitation. Her gaze searched his in the dim lighting, her own expression incredibly guileless and filled with candid desire. "I want to be with you. I...I care about you, more than I probably should considering this is all we'll have together, but I can't change how I feel or pretend it doesn't exist." Her free hand charted a path up his arm, across his shoulder, and curled around the nape of his neck. "And I think you need this as much as I do."

Jackson closed his eyes as a shudder ripped through him. Desperately, he tried to summon the willpower to refuse this moment, and her. Hell, he had no idea what he was doing anymore, only knew he wanted the closeness and connection she was offering him. The openness and honesty, even if it was about sex. No, *making love,* he amended. He was too emotionally invested for it to be anything less.

Her lips brushed his, as sweet as the promise of heaven, while her thumb slipped over the silky head of his penis in an unbearable, erotic caress that pushed him closer to the point of no return. "*Please,*" she breathed against his mouth.

That one word shattered the last of his restraint, causing a flood of need to overwhelm him. With a groan of raw hunger he pressed her against the wall beneath the shower spigot, crushing her soft breasts against his chest and nestling his erection between her slightly parted thighs. Burying his hands into her wet hair, he angled her mouth beneath his and captured her lips in a ravenous kiss she wholeheartedly welcomed. He filled her mouth with the velvet heat of his tongue, plunging deep and thrusting hard, unable to get enough of the intoxicating taste of her. She was addictive, to his libido, his heart and his emotions.

His need clawed at him, consuming his every thought, making him forget everything but this woman clinging to him and how much he ached to lose himself deep inside her, to be completely surrounded by her sultry heat and generous body. Despite every effort, he couldn't fight the need any longer and knew the culmination of the past few days would be nothing short of incendiary.

Her tongue dueled with his, and he pushed his hips forward, sliding the rigid length of his penis against her dewy, feminine folds, slick with desire. She gasped into his mouth, then issued a long, wild moan as she moved in counterpoint to his teasing foray, rotating her hips in slow, maddeningly erotic circles that caused a scorching heat to unfurl in his belly and radiate outward. One more tantalizing stroke and he'd be so far gone there'd be no stopping the climax that was beckoning, and he wasn't ready for any of this to end just yet.

He dragged his mouth from hers and managed to put a few inches between them. Physically they were no longer touching, but visually he followed the caress of the water sluicing down her body. "We have to slow down," he said, gulping deep breaths.

She blinked up at him slumberously, her lips pink

and swollen from his kiss and her skin warm, wet and glowing. "Then how about we play for a little bit?" She reached for the liquid soap, but before she could grab the bottle he intercepted the move.

He'd never last with her hands all over him. Stroking him intimately. Teasing mercilessly. Exploring shamelessly. No, that's what *he* planned to do. "I'm already clean, so allow me the pleasure of washing you."

The suggestion brightened her eyes with excitement. "I'm all yours," she murmured.

Releasing the massage type showerhead from its hook, he placed it in her hand. He grinned as she looked at him in bewilderment.

"I'll wash, and you rinse when I tell you," he told her.

Her pale, smooth shoulders lifted in a shrug. "Okay," she said easily—too easily, and Jackson knew she had no idea what he had in store for her.

But that was part of the fun, and if this night was all he had with Alexis he wanted to enjoy and savor every moment of it. He soaped up his hands, made her turn around, and glided his slick palms across her back and down her spine, massaging her supple skin with his fingertips. She splayed her free hand on the wall to support herself, and her head fell forward as a groan of pleasure caught in her throat.

His hands continued on, cupping and kneading her buttocks. Instinctively she arched her bottom toward him, offering a sexual position he'd always been extremely fond of, but he managed, just barely, to resist that particular temptation.

"Go ahead and rinse," he said, his voice rough with arousal and restraint.

She brought the shower spray to her shoulders and let the water flow down her back. He followed the suds' slippery journey downward with his hands just as an excuse to touch her, and once her neck was no longer soapy he pressed his mouth there and licked the moisture from her skin.

She shivered, and he gradually eased her around to face him as he once again soaped up his hands. Their gazes met and held as he splayed his frothy fingers on her upper chest. In excruciatingly slow increments he let them drift lower, skimming his palms over her plump, straining breasts, then plucking and rolling her nipples between his thumb and fingers until they were hard as pebbles.

Her lips parted on a languorous sigh, and he leaned forward and kissed her waiting mouth, slow and deep and lazy this time...as slow and lazy as the hands sliding down her belly. His thumbs toyed with her navel until she squirmed, then moved on to span her waist and hips. He didn't have to ask her to rinse this time, and as the water cascaded down her body his mouth followed the path. His lips slid along her arched throat to the pulse pattering in the delicate hollow of her collarbone. His soft kisses alternated between delicate laps of his tongue and arousing nips of his teeth that made her moan, and fired his blood.

He gave her wet breasts and the stiff, sensitive peaks the same lavish attention, and she drizzled the water over his back, sharing the warmth, while her other hand slicked across his shoulders and down his arms. He nuzzled the swell of her breasts and swirled his tongue over the erect tips, flicking and teasing before suckling one crest deep into his mouth. A frustrated, mewling sound escaped her when he moved on, scattering kisses over her stomach and dipping his tongue into her belly button before working his way back up to her mouth.

Her eyes were feverish, her face flushed with longing, and her whole body trembled from the erotic play of his hands and mouth. "Jackson..."

He shook his head and pressed two fingers over her damp lips. "I'm not done yet," he rasped.

Nudging her legs apart with his foot, he knelt in front of her, bringing him eye level with the breathtaking sight of her femininity. His mouth went dry and his stomach muscles tightened. Droplets of water clung to the moist black curls like morning dew, and the faint, aroused scent of her filled the deep breath that expanded his lungs and made his blood surge through his veins.

He started with her feet, working his way up, coating her with silky bubbles from her firm calves to her knees, to her silken thighs...and there he was again, enticed and beguiled and enthralled by the most intimate part of her. Hunger sliced through him, and the pangs had nothing to do with food and everything to do with Alexis.

Unable to stop himself, he slipped his fingers between her legs, a featherlight whisper of sensation as he outlined the juncture of her thighs. Her skin quivered, her breathing deepened, and without being asked, and with shaking hands, she lifted the sprayer to her belly to rinse off the soap. He watched, entranced, as the white foam slithered down her thighs, her calves, her feet, and disappeared down the drain.

But she'd missed that tender, sensitive place between her legs, and he wasn't about to be denied this erotic pleasure. Wasn't about to let her hide and be modest now. With a hand on her stomach, he gently pushed her back so her spine was braced against the wall. Lifting her left knee, he draped her leg over his broad shoulder, opening her wide. His hand slid down the back of her thigh and smoothed over her buttocks. He dipped his long fingers in the crease of her bottom and touched her slick heat, then used his thumbs to part her softly swelled flesh, exposing all of her to his gaze.

She gasped in startled surprise, but didn't protest his bold caress or the shocking position, no matter how vulnerable either might have made her feel. She trusted him, and that knowledge humbled him in ways he didn't want to analyze at the moment.

His gaze traveled upward, past her pert breasts and meeting her wide eyes, which were filled with a higher level of excitement. "You missed a few spots." His voice was husky, but threaded with an unmistakable dare.

She swallowed hard, and silently accepted his sexy challenge. Lifting the nozzle, she aimed the surge of water against her thigh, then slowly moved the stream upward, until the vibrating jets met that feminine flash point.

At the first contact of pulsing water her body jerked in response. Her head fell back on a soft moan, her lashes fluttered closed, and she bit her bottom lip between her teeth. Her breathing grew ragged and short, then escalated in tempo as the pleasure intensified. The uninhibited way she arched toward the pelting liquid, combined with the lusty sounds she made in the back of her throat, all blended together to tighten the knot of desire and need coiling within Jackson.

Then all he knew was that *he* wanted to give her that release, wanted to taste the richness of her climax on his tongue when she came. Unable to be a passive bystander to her satisfaction, he pushed her hand away and replaced the torrent of water with the intimate suction of his mouth. She shuddered at the hot stroke of his tongue in needful places, and dropped the sprayer when two fingers dipped, swirled, then delved deeply into the incredible tightness of her woman's sheath. Her hands, now free, raked through his hair as he ravished her. He was wicked and ruthless, and she was gloriously wanton, undulating and riding with the rhythm he set.

He pushed her higher. She whimpered and begged in the sweetest way, and he finally gave her what she ached for and what he'd withheld until this moment. He increased the pressure of his mouth and tongue, the glide of his fingers, and she came apart fast and furiously, her body shaking and convulsing in wild abandon.

A cry of completion escaped her, and once her rippling contractions ebbed he stood back up so she'd have something to cling to. She wrapped her arms around his neck and he crushed her limp, satiated body between the wall and his hard, thoroughly aroused body. Without preamble, he captured her mouth with his, stealing her breath and sharing the taste of her in a kiss that was deep and rapacious, yet soulful and sensual.

When he finally let them both up for air, she held onto him in a daze, her eyes glazed with unfettered passion and something far more sentimental. She touched his tight jaw with tentative fingers, then skimmed her thumb over his bottom lip, damp from her and their shared kiss.

"I need *you*," she whispered.

Her heartfelt invocation unleashed something powerfully primitive within Jackson, a fiercely protective yet infinitely tender reaction. No one had ever *needed* him before, at least not in such an honest, emotional way. He stared at her guileless expression, believing her, falling for her, forgetting everything but *her* and this poignant moment that would change everything between them.

She swallowed, then said the words that were his final undoing, "Jackson, make love to me."

Yes.

Undeniable urgency arched between them, an accumulation of all the foreplay they'd endured. Without another indecisive thought Jackson shut off the water and they stumbled dripping wet into the small adjoining cabin, illuminated by the dim lighting of the lamp secured to the wall. Arms and legs tangled as he pressed her down onto the middle of the soft comforter covering the double bed that dominated the area. He caught a quick, appreciative glimpse of her spread out beneath him, all gentle curves and soft, giving woman before he moved over her, his thighs pushing hers wide apart to accommodate his hips. Their skin met, wet and slick and feverish with desire. Entwining their fingers and pressing their palms together, he folded their arms above her head, joining them in every way but the most intimate.

Luminescent eyes stared up at him as he pushed the head of his erection inside her a few inches. She gasped, and he groaned as her body enveloped the tip of his shaft, snug and silky hot. And then he abruptly stopped his tumble toward bliss as he came to his senses and realized what he was about to do. He needed this connection with Alexis as much as his life depended on his next breath, but the joke was on him. No matter how much he wanted to be with her this way, he'd deliberately planned it so they *couldn't* make love because he didn't have any protection with him.

He swore silently, and the loss that instantly consumed him was excruciating. Before what little was left of his control vanished, he moved up and back to separate their bodies, but before he could withdraw from the warm haven of being inside her, she anticipated his intent and locked her legs around the back of his thighs, stopping his retreat.

Her fingers clenched around his, and she shook her head frantically. "Jackson, no..."

His heart squeezed tight with regret, and he hated that he'd brought them this far, only to have to end the exquisite moment they both needed with equal intensity. "Sweetheart...I don't have any condoms."

It took a few seconds for his comment to register. "It's okay," she finally said, her well-kissed lips softening with a smile. "You don't need one."

He opened his mouth to argue just as their conversation about physicals and a clean bill of health came back to him, making him realize that she must have come prepared for this. Relief poured through him, and then the only thing that mattered was making her his. She lifted her head and seduced him with a tongue-tangling French kiss, and he followed her lead, lowering his weight back on top of her. With little coaxing, he pressed his hips forward, stretching her with his length and breadth as he sank deeper and deeper inside her.

Buried to the hilt with Alexis moving restlessly beneath him and making sexy, impatient sounds in the back of her throat, Jackson couldn't stop the mindless sensations engulfing him. He began to thrust as his body demanded him to—long, hot strokes that sent an almost desperate, frantic need sizzling through him. He pumped harder, faster, furiously, and she turned to pure wildfire beneath him.

His release came swiftly, and at the moment of crisis he tore his mouth from hers. With a deep, guttural groan, he surrendered to the friction, the wet heat, and the way Alexis gave to him so selflessly while asking nothing of him in return. And as he pressed his face against the crook of her neck after emptying his heart and soul into her body, he realized for the first time in his life he felt alive and wanted...*just for himself.*

9

THE BREAK OF DAWN came much too quickly for Alexis. How could she wish to see the end of a night that ranked as one of the most sensual and decadent experiences of her life? The kind of cherished keepsake she'd hoped for when she'd booked her trip to Seductive Fantasy.

A contented sigh drifted past her parted lips as she snuggled closer to Jackson's side. The musky, masculine heat of him, the press of their bodies, and the intoxicating scent of their lovemaking all mingled, making her skin tingle in renewed awareness. And just that easily, the wanting started all over again, even though they'd satisfied every erotic craving they'd had for each other during the course of the night.

Gently, she rested her hand over his heart, enjoying the quiet moment to think and luxuriate in this man who'd made her feel so whole and complete in such a short span of time. She could feel the steady beat beneath her palm and the rise and fall of his chest. His breathing was deep and even in slumber, and she smiled to herself, feeling equally exhausted and sated.

Though their night together had been equal parts give and take, she was certain she'd succeeded in giving Jackson pleasurable memories to replace the bad ones that had consumed him up on deck last night. In return, he'd shown her just how wonderful and exciting making love could be—with the right person. And sometime during the course of the evening she'd fallen irrevocably in love with Jackson Witt. He was exactly the kind of sincere, sexy man she hadn't known she'd been searching for until she'd found him.

Her lashes fluttered closed as her heart gave a small, painful twist beneath her breast. While she accepted her emotions, embraced them even, they came without demands. Not only did she still not know Jackson's reasons for being here on the island, or even how she fit into his fantasy, there had never been any promises between them, other than the promise of pleasure, which they'd fulfilled in spades. A commitment or future together was highly unlikely considering they lived thousands of miles apart.

But what if she discovered she was pregnant?

Undoubtedly, conceiving a child had been part of her fantasy, but that had been the last thing on her mind last night. Her only concern had been to make Jackson feel more than the pain of his past, to give him something to trust and believe in—*her*. Now she had to consider the new, emotional consequences of a pregnancy.

Making her decision came easily, based purely on love. If she discovered she was pregnant, she owed it to Jackson to tell him, without demands, without strings, or any kind of expectations from him. She acknowledged the flaws in her original plan to conceive a baby, and how wrong she'd been to think she could get pregnant without informing the baby's father. Regardless of her original plan, there was no way she could take something as important as a child away from Jackson when he'd been without so much in his life.

But until she was able to confirm in a few weeks that she'd become pregnant, there was nothing she could do. She only had today and tomorrow with Jackson and she intended to make the best of their time together and make sure he knew exactly how she felt about him by the end of their vacation.

Jackson stirred next to her, the muscles in his arms flexing as he rolled to his side and tucked her against him so their bodies were aligned—her spine to his chest, her bottom to his groin, all the way down to their entwined legs. She waited for him to say or do something to indicate he was awake, but he was obviously still trying to catch up on his sleep.

Alex relaxed in his embrace and savored the moment, which would pass too quickly, she knew. Needing something to mark this memory in her mind forever, she closed her eyes and whispered the words crowding her heart, "I love you," and wasn't at all surprised that the sentiment slipped from her lips as naturally as if she'd been saying them to Jackson for years, instead of just a day.

I LOVE YOU.

Five hours later, Alexis's words still rang clear in Jackson's mind. Now back on the island, he was following the path to his cottage after dropping Alexis off at the hotel and promising to meet her in an hour for lunch. Her declaration wove through him like the sweetest promise, yet compounded the guilt brought on by his charade. He'd been on the brink of waking up when he'd heard her soft, sleep-husky voice speak those three life-altering words. While at first he'd thought he'd been dreaming, the reality of it had quickly hit home with a jolt.

She loved him. He'd gotten exactly what he'd wanted from his personal fantasy—Alexis's emotional involvement. All that remained was for him to tell her who he really was, then walk away. The revenge he'd originally sought against Alexis was his, so why did he feel like the lowest form of life instead of victorious?

He knew the answer to his question, and had been struggling against his own emotions for days. Somewhere along the way, his thirst for vengeance had gotten tangled up with his feelings for Alexis and she'd become too important to him to hurt so callously. He could no more spurn the gift she'd given him, of love and acceptance, any more than he believed her directly responsible for the theft of technology from his company. He didn't have physical proof yet of her innocence, but his gut told him otherwise. And now that he knew Alexis intimately, he could honestly say that piracy just didn't fit with her generous, steadfast personality.

In his initial anger, and having been burned before, he'd acted rashly and without giving Alexis the benefit of the doubt. But he gave that to her now.

And all he could do was try and rectify the situation and what he'd done...and pray that he didn't lose Alexis in the process.

With his insides churning in turmoil, he withdrew his key card from his back pocket, slipped it into the mechanism on his cottage door and stepped inside the cool, spacious beach suite. No matter how he analyzed the situation, there was no avoiding her eventually discovering his true identity. Alexis wasn't stupid and would quickly put two and two together and realize his true motives for being on Seductive Fantasy. There was nothing he could do about any of those complications now...except do the respectable thing and opt for good old-fashioned honesty. When and how was another issue, he thought with a reluctant grimace, but divulging the truth was something he had to do if he wanted any chance of salvaging their relationship.

Their relationship. He expected the notion of wanting something more lasting with Alexis to strike fear into his heart, but the only thing that rattled him was the thought of her *hating* him once everything was out in the open. And she'd have every right to despise him after the way he'd deceived her. Having been on the receiving end of betrayal many times in his life, he knew the pain that accompanied it.

Ignoring the pounding in his temples and the ache in his chest, he picked up the phone in the living room and punched out the number for Mike's private line back in Atlanta. His request for Mike to do a thorough background check on Fred Hobson to try to gather incriminating evidence against the man would be a start in rectifying his mistake with Alexis.

"I HEARD there's going to be a farewell party tonight," Alexis said as she pushed her fork into the chicken salad she'd ordered for lunch at the outdoor café facing the atrium. "Are you up for that?"

Jackson gave her question serious consideration as he chewed a bite of his hamburger and forced an appetite that was nonexistent. Was he up for mingling in a crowd of people and sharing his last few hours with Alexis with strangers? No. All he wanted, at this very moment and through tomorrow afternoon when they were scheduled to leave, was to selfishly spend every second with her *alone*...sharing more about each other, touching her soft skin, kissing her sensual lips, *making love to her*. Yeah, especially that.

His conscience ruthlessly kicked in, grounding his meandering thoughts. For as much as he'd love to spend the next twenty-four hours indulging in nothing but erotic pleasures with her, he knew they couldn't be intimate again until they talked and aired everything between them. He couldn't allow himself to add another offense to his already long list of transgressions. Not if he wanted a chance at something more with her. And he did, in ways that made him feel nearly desperate to gain her forgiveness before she discovered what he'd done.

"Hello. Earth to Jackson," Alexis teased, bringing him back to the present.

"Sorry 'bout that." He shook his head and glanced across the table, taking in her animated expression, her glowing skin, and how she'd blossomed into a sensual creature this past week just for him. "I was hoping we could spend tonight alone."

A sexy, excited gleam sparked in her eyes. "I like that idea, too. A whole bunch." She took a drink of her iced tea and dabbed her napkin across her lips. "We could spend the evening at your place, watch the sun set, and afterward have a moonlight picnic on the beach."

There was no way he could refuse her request or burst her enthusiastic bubble with a "no." Not on their last night together. "That sounds perfect." And during that picnic they'd *talk*...not touch, or kiss, or make love.

"*You're* perfect, Jackson," she said in response. She'd grown suddenly serious, though there was a serene quality about her features that grabbed at something deep within him and tugged hard. "Merrilee said you'd be everything I asked for on this vacation, and more. And you are."

And soon she'd learn that he was more than she ever expected! "I feel the same way," he replied, compelled to share that bit of honesty with her, even though he was certain she'd believe his words a lie once she knew the truth.

She fiddled with the knife tucked next to her salad plate. "You know, there's something that's been on my mind that I'd like to say," she said tentatively.

His entire body tensed, wondering where this conversation would lead. Wondering if maybe she'd be bold enough to express her feelings for him out loud and while he was wide awake. As casually as he could manage, he pushed his half-eaten hamburger aside and leaned back in his chair. "What's been on your mind?"

She ducked her head, a slight flush coloring her cheeks. "Well, we've seemed to hit it off incredibly well, and I was hoping that we might be able to pursue whatever it is between us once we leave the resort." Her eyes met his expectantly, her feelings for him reflecting clear and true in the depths. "I know we live on opposite ends of the country, and long-distance relationships are difficult, but maybe we could find a way to make it work?"

Yes. His chest expanded and burned as he drew a deep, fortifying breath, knowing he couldn't offer her promises because he didn't have the right to make them. At least not yet. "Alexis—"

Insecurities promptly filled her gaze, and she held up a slender hand to stop what she believed or feared would be a rejection. "Don't give me an answer right now," she said, her voice soft and slightly husky. "Just think about it, Jackson."

A tremulous laugh escaped her, and she continued in a rush. "I mean, I really have no idea what your fantasy is, and it might be a bit presumptuous of me to think that this week has been just as special for you as it's been for me. And if that's the case and this is all one-sided, then I'd rather wait until tomorrow for this wonderful fantasy to end. And if it ends with goodbye, then I'll accept that. And if you find that you'd like to see where all this leads, then you already know how I feel."

I love you. Oh, yeah, he knew exactly how she felt,

and right now, he didn't deserve to be on the receiving end of that heartfelt emotion. The only thing he had going in his favor was the twenty-four hours he still had to convince her he was worthy of everything she'd given him this past week.

"Ms. Baylor?"

Startled by the intrusion of a third voice when her sole focus had been on Jackson, she transferred her gaze to the concierge who'd approached their table, a portable phone in his hand. "Yes, I'm Ms. Baylor," she said, her expression curious.

"I apologize for interrupting your lunch, but I have an urgent call for you from a Dennis Merrick. I saw you come into the café through the lobby, and he was adamant about not leaving a voice mail message if he could talk to you personally."

Worry immediately creased her brows as she reached for the phone. "I'll take the call. Thank you." Frowning, she tucked the unit up against her ear. "Dennis, is everything okay?"

She was quiet for what seemed like hours instead of minutes to Jackson as her VP talked, and as she listened he watched her expression shift from worry, to disbelief, to outright anger.

Then came her heated reply. "I can't believe that Fred Hobson worked for Extreme Software! How is that *possible*?" Her incredulity was nearly tangible.

Oh, it was possible all right. Jackson visibly winced, but Alexis was too caught up in her own turmoil to notice his discomfort. Obviously, her lawyers hadn't wasted time in investigating Hobson's background. And though he was a day late and a dollar short in his own attempt to find out the connection between Fred, Gametek and his company, relief poured through him that his instincts this past week about the woman across from him had been accurate.

She dragged shaking fingers through her hair, pushing the thick, silky strands away from her shocked expression. "I knew he'd gone to Atlanta to live after he quit Gametek, but his last place of employment was for an electronics company when I rehired him," she said adamantly, confirming Jackson's suspicions that she had no knowledge of Fred's piracy. She buried her face in her hand and groaned in distress. "Oh, God, Dennis, what a mess...."

Alexis suddenly sat up straight in her seat, listening to Dennis intently. Her gaze flew to Jackson's, and her lips parted in a swift intake of air. Immediately, his stomach cramped and his skin prickled with the kind of foreboding he couldn't escape or shake.

"What did you say the owner's name of Extreme Software was?" she asked, her voice a barely audible croak of sound.

Jackson swore beneath his breath, knowing his time was up, and so was his cover.

The color in her face drained away, accentuating her huge blue eyes that brimmed with devastation as realization dawned. A shudder racked her body as if she had to forcibly suppress a swell of nausea. Betrayal, he knew all too well, had a way of making a person physically ill.

"Dennis...I've got to go. I'll call you later." She

disconnected the line, set the phone on the table next to her plate and closed her eyes as if to shut him out. Jackson had never felt more alone, so afraid of losing something vitally important to him.

"What have I done?" she whispered more to herself than him, the words escaping on a tangle of emotion.

He didn't think she'd appreciate him supplying the answer. She'd fallen in love with him, had given him her body and her heart and the essence of her soul, all three of which he'd come to cherish. But she wouldn't see it that way, and he couldn't blame her for believing that what had happened between them was all a sham. He didn't know what to say at that moment, so he waited for her to get past her initial shock to see what would happen.

She did, eventually. When she opened her eyes again she was incredibly composed and frustratingly formal. The smile that edged up the corner of her mouth was cool, matching the frost in her unreadable eyes. Gone was the warm woman who'd been so soft and sweet and giving in his arms last night.

"It's nice to finally meet the man behind the complaint filed against Gametek for copyright infringement," she finally said in an even tone, as if they were discussing the weather on the island and not the destruction he'd nearly wrought on her company. The emotional destruction he'd wrought on *her*.

He reached across the table to grasp the hand resting on the portable phone, needing that connection, but she snatched her arm back before he could touch her. Without another word, she scraped her chair back, stood, then with her spine straight and her head held proud, she started for the atrium.

Cursing a blue streak and not caring who heard him, Jackson followed her out to the lush garden area and caught up to her near one of the waterfalls. He knew better than to touch her, knew he no longer had the right, so he took a more formidable approach and stepped right in front of her path and stopped. His bold move forced her to come to an abrupt halt or crash into him.

Her chin raised a fraction. "If you don't let me pass, I'll call for security."

He blew out a harsh breath, having never anticipated a stubborn streak in Alexis. At any other time he would have admired the trait. Now it just got in the way of him trying to reach her. "Alexis, let me explain..." As if there was any explanation for his seductive revenge, or any excuse for the way he'd trampled on her heart by not being honest much, much sooner.

Much to his surprise, she didn't rebuff him and his attempt to justify his actions. Or call for security. "Go ahead, Mr. Witt. Explain," she said calmly.

He would have felt much more relieved to see her rant and rave, slug him in the midsection even, something to purge the fury he knew she had to be feeling. "Yes, it's true I initially booked this fantasy because I believed you were responsible for stealing from my company the design you needed to complete your software for *Zantoid*." He'd spent the past week fabricating truths, and he refused to lie now. "And when all the facts were laid out in front of me, it looked like you used Fred Hobson to do it. He worked for your company in San Diego, came to work for me in Atlanta, then quit Extreme Software to return to Gametek. It looked like far more than a mere coincidence when Gametek announced a gaming software program that isn't possible without *my* technology."

She crossed her arms over her chest and waited, not denying his claim or defending herself or her company as she had every right to do.

He swallowed the swell of emotion that seemed to choke off his airway and forced himself to continue. "I found out that you were going to be vacationing here, and I saw it as the perfect opportunity to exact my own revenge before the courts took over."

Pain briefly glimmered in her eyes, but she quickly blinked it away. "A private, *seductive* revenge," she said, pushing him to admit the truth out loud.

"Yes." He braced his fisted hands on his hips, resisting the impulse to reach out to her. "I've spent my life feeling used, mainly for what I could provide, and I felt as though this was the last straw for me. I'd been pushed too far, and one time too many, and...I just snapped. I wasn't about to let someone else take advantage of me again, and use *my* technology to further their company's financial gain. And so I decided that this time I'd take something from that other person...from *you*."

She shrugged impassively. "Then I'd say you got exactly what you wanted, Jackson."

He flinched at her standoffish tone, but continued with what he wanted to say before she decided she didn't care to hear anything more and walked away. "Like you, I got more than I bargained for. I knew from the first moment I met you that you were different and not at all what I'd imagined, and I've been struggling all week long with my conscience. I fell for you, Alexis, in ways that scare the hell out of me. You know more about me than anyone I know. And then suddenly everything seemed so complicated because I didn't want to hurt you, but I knew eventually you'd find out who I was."

A skeptical look crossed her features. She didn't believe him and his feelings for her, and he felt helpless to convince her otherwise. She stared at him for a long minute, and he waited for some sign of forgiveness and understanding. He received neither.

"For your information, and whether you believe me or not, Fred Hobson stole that technology from your company without my knowledge." She stated her facts in a cool, precise voice.

"I know that now, and I *do* believe you." His statement, while pure truth, was meager compensation for his week-long deceit.

"And when he presented it to my team of designers and told us that he'd created it himself, there was no reason for us not to believe him, and he obviously thought he'd never get caught." She stated her facts as if they were sitting in a boardroom discussing business. "According to Dennis, Fred will be prosecuted, but as the president of Gametek, I profusely apologize for any emotional or financial damages this might have caused you or your company."

The sound of the waterfall behind them echoed like the roar of blood in his ears as his temper raised a notch. Did she really think he was more concerned about *damages*? "I don't give a damn about any of that!" he said through clenched teeth.

His outburst didn't even startle her, which infuriated him even more.

"How can you not give a damn?" she asked benignly. "That gaming chip obviously meant a lot to you to go to such extremes."

Her reasonable tone nearly sent him over the edge. "Dammit, Alexis, I can't stand this!"

She blinked at him. "Stand what?"

"This. *You*." He waved an impatient hand between them as he tried to explain. "I want some kind of emotional reaction from you. Anger. Rage. *Something*. Even slapping me would be preferable to this cool attitude of yours."

She sighed, the sound tinged with undeniable sadness. "What do I have to be upset about, Jackson? You gave *me* exactly what I came here for: a hot, illicit affair. I couldn't have asked for a better, more attentive lover than you've been."

He sucked in a harsh breath. Oh, that sliced deep and straight to his heart, but he deserved the verbal slap if she wasn't going to indulge in a physical one.

"I knew there were risks when I agreed to this fantasy," she went on judiciously. "And I accepted them, so I have no one to blame but myself for letting things go as far as they did."

Feeling desperate to reach past her calm facade, he decided to be ruthless. "What about what you said back there at the café? About me and about us?"

"I said those things to Jackson Witt, my fantasy man. And I'm not sure I know *who* the real Jackson Witt is anymore." Her voice was tight with regret, and though he could have sworn he saw a fleeting glimpse of moisture in her eyes, no tears appeared. She drew a deep, stabilizing breath. "Now, if you'll excuse me, I have some business to take care of."

This time when she stepped around him, he let her past, but he couldn't stop from torturing himself even more; he turned around to watch her go. An excruciating sense of loss consumed him as she walked through the open glass slider that led to the lobby. And as the door slid shut behind her, Jackson was struck with the irony that *she* was the one to walk away, and *he* was the one left with his emotions in shambles.

A PAINFUL SOB caught in the back of Alex's throat and the tears she hadn't shed in front of Jackson now burned her eyes. She blinked them back, refusing to fall apart when she needed to face Merrilee to put in a request to leave the island a day early. There was no way she could remain on Seductive Fantasy and face the possibility of running into Jackson again. Everything either one of them could have said had been aired out in the atrium.

With effort, she pushed her misery aside until later, to purge when she was alone and could release her anguish without any witnesses. At a young age she'd learned to be tough and strong...and she'd learned to be alone, too, no matter how strong the desire was otherwise. She'd live through this catastrophe, just as she'd survived her parents' death and life's other jarring episodes.

Swallowing convulsively, she headed past the shops in the lobby to Merrilee's office, which was located down a corridor next to the registration area. She prayed that the other woman was in, and if she wasn't, she'd have her paged and tracked down. This was undoubtedly an emergency, considering her breaking heart depended on putting as many miles between her and Jackson as possible.

It had been her own fault for falling in love with him, but she couldn't regret her feelings for Jackson or even her fantasy, which had been fulfilled beyond her wildest expectations. She even understood his reasons for initially seeking revenge and believing her responsible for the piracy of his technology. But it was Jackson's reluctance to believe and trust in *himself* that had Alex tied up in knots inside.

She knew he cared, even believed his heartfelt confession about how he'd fallen for her. The feelings he'd let loose out on the boat, coupled with their intense lovemaking and his ultimate surrender, had been too genuine to be feigned. Unfortunately he was too wrapped up in past betrayals to believe that a woman could accept him for who he was. Because of that, and until he learned to trust in his emotions, Alex knew he'd always look for ulterior motives when it came to the female gender and would be unable to commit himself to a woman. And if he couldn't trust her, then they had nothing together except the memories they'd made this week.

A shuddering breath escaped her, and she strengthened her composure as she turned down the hallway to Merrilee's office. She honestly didn't know what to think or feel other than misery and confusion. Because of what she'd revealed at the café, Jackson knew how she felt about him, and if he truly meant what he'd said about falling for her, too, then he'd have to trust in those emotions she'd seen glimpses of earlier, trust in *himself*, and ultimately prove it.

10

MERRILEE FOUND Jackson in the resort's fitness center working out on the Stairmaster machine at a brutal pace. His face was contorted in fierce concentration, and the muscles in his arms and legs bunched with every quick, hard step he took. No doubt he was burning off the remorse engulfing him, or at least she hoped that's what he was doing, because he didn't look like a man revelling in victory. Thank goodness!

Without hesitation, she wound her way around the bulky equipment, weight sets and other patrons until she stood in front of Jackson's machine. He eyed her approach warily, as well he should. She wasn't at all happy with him at the moment and hoped during the course of their conversation he'd exhibit a few redeeming qualities that would restore her faith in him. While she didn't appreciate that he'd lied to her to gain access to one of her guests for personal reasons, she had to believe that Alexis hadn't been the only one who'd invested emotions into her week-long fantasy. Every time she'd seen the two of them together they'd both seemed very attracted and completely in tune with each other in a way that couldn't be feigned.

"I take it you're looking for me?" he said between

pants of breath as he slowly brought the machine to a stop.

She kept her expression stern. "Considering we have a bit of a problem with the fantasy you officially requested and what you had in mind personally, I think you and I need to talk."

Stepping off the Stairmaster unit, he swiped at the sweat on his face with the towel draped around his neck, his mouth stretching into a grim line. "Alexis spoke with you." It wasn't a question, but rather a statement.

She took the guilt reflecting in his intense blue eyes as a very good sign. She'd talked to Alexis and learned *everything*, from Jackson's deceit to Alexis's deepest emotions toward this man in front of her. Despite what he'd done to her, Alexis admitted that she still loved him, but the next move was solely up to Jackson.

"You sound surprised, which you really shouldn't be. She wanted to leave the island a day early, and I wasn't about to let her go until I knew the reason why."

Undiluted panic etched his handsome features. "She's gone?"

She was gratified to see that he was upset about that and let his dismay linger a bit longer. That particular emotion bolstered her optimism toward him, made her believe that there was hope for a happy ending between these two after all. *If* Jackson was willing to work for it.

She headed toward the terrace overlooking the beach adjoining the gym, away from prying eyes and ears. This wasn't a conversation she wanted to share with other guests. Jackson was only a few paces behind, seemingly interested in whatever she had to say that pertained to Alexis.

She turned around at the railing and addressed him. "Did you really expect her to stay once she discovered what you did?"

His mouth opened, snapped shut, and then he gave a resigned sighed. "Honestly, I'd hoped that if I gave her a little time alone she'd—"

"Come to her senses after the way you betrayed her?"

He frowned at the extra digs she was tossing into the mix, but she wanted him to understand that she knew exactly what he'd done, and she wasn't pleased about it.

He gripped both ends of the towel around his neck. "I'm already feeling lower than a snake, thank you very much."

"That's good to know."

His frown deepened. "I thought after everything was out in the open between Alexis and me that some time alone would help her put everything into perspective and she'd realize that while my fantasy had begun as a revenge, it hadn't ended that way. Not at all."

His honest confession was exactly what Merrilee wanted to hear, but she needed to know a few more things. "Tell me something, Jackson. Was there any truth in the fantasy you told me? The one about wanting to find a woman you can open up to and

trust? Or was that all just a ruse to get you on the island and close to Alexis?"

He closed his eyes for a moment, and when they
opened again they were filled with misery. "Initially,
it was all a pretense. But as I spent more and more
time with Alexis, I came to see that there was more
truth to that fantasy than I'd ever realized. I meant
what I said when I told you that my relationships
with women have been lacking, and I've been betrayed one time too many, and I thought Alexis was
yet another woman that was after a piece of me. But
I instinctively knew after the first few nights with her
that she was different, and I did open up to her in
ways I've never opened up to another woman. So in
some ways, that fantasy was fulfilled in ways I never
expected."

Merrilee crossed her arms over her chest. "So, not
everything was a farce between the two of you
then?" She had to know.

"No." He shook his head. "In fact, the only thing
that wasn't honest and true between us was my
omission that I was the owner of Extreme Software,
the company that filed a complaint against her company. Everything else was as real as it gets."

She tilted her head and regarded him speculati-
vely. So, he'd fallen in love, too. He might not realize just how deeply, but Merrilee considered herself
an expert on the matter and she could see the emotion in his eyes, see it on his face. The sentiment
touched something inside her that reminded her of
the love she'd once shared with Charlie and lost
much too quickly. She didn't want these two people

who needed one another so much to lose one of life's most precious gifts. But someone had to give in this situation, and she got the distinct impression from Alexis that it wouldn't be her, since the other woman had told her that Jackson knew how she felt about him. The question was, was Jackson willing to take a few risks to gain a lifetime of happiness? It was a decision only he could make.

"Merrilee..." His deep voice drew her back, and she met his sincere gaze. "I owe you an apology for misleading you."

"Yes, you do."

A wry grin canted the corner of his mouth. "I'm very sorry." At her accepting nod, he added, "And I apologize for using Alexis, as well."

Merrilee saw this as her last opportunity to give him a push in the right direction, and she could only hope that Jackson didn't let this woman slip out of his life. "I think you owe *her* a whole lot more than an apology."

"I TOLD YOU to be careful what you wish for, buddy," Mike said, then tipped his bottle of beer to his lips for a long drink.

Jackson grunted in response as he wiped condensation from his own beer bottle and stared at his friend across their table at a local hangout. He didn't need Mike's "I told you so" to add to his grief, but he deserved it nonetheless. Yeah, Jackson had gotten exactly what he'd wished for on Seductive Fantasy, and Mike had been right on the money when he'd told Jackson that the cost of this particular fantasy could be a personal one for him, too. He'd gone to Seductive Fantasy looking to take something away from Alexis, and he'd ended up taking something away from himself, instead—a woman who accepted and loved him for the man he was and expected nothing else.

Jackson never could have anticipated just how personal the stakes would be. But now he knew, and he'd spent way too much time berating himself for his actions and wishing he'd handled things much, much differently. Never would he have predicted that his fantasy would backfire on him and leave him feeling emptier than he'd ever felt before.

Nearly three weeks had passed since Jackson had left the island resort and returned home to Atlanta. In an attempt to make amends, he'd sent Alexis a huge bouquet of flowers with a note of apology, and never heard a word from her. It had been a cowardly way of handling things, but his biggest fear was that she'd grown to despise him, and that was something he couldn't bear to hear in her voice if he called her. And since she hadn't responded to his overture in any way whatsoever, he'd assumed that it was best if he left her alone and stepped out of her life completely.

He'd received a settlement offer today from Gametek meant to smooth out the legal aspects of his original complaint, even though he'd immediately dropped it upon returning back home. But Alexis obviously believed she owed him something more on a business level, and that irked him, too.

"You'll never believe what I received today," he said to Mike, who looked at him with raised brows above eyes full of interest. "A six-figure, out-of-court settlement offer from Gametek."

"Wow." Mike finished off his beer while he considered Jackson's comment and what it implied. "So, what are you going to do now?"

He didn't think twice. "Reject the offer, of course. I don't want her money. As far as Alexis is concerned, I don't know," he replied honestly. "Any suggestions, oh, wise one?"

Mike shrugged. "The answer seems pretty simple and straightforward enough to me. You go to San Diego and face her and find out if there's anything left to reconcile in this mess you made of things."

His stomach churned with indecision, though Mike's suggestion had been preying on his mind more and more lately. Yet the more time that lapsed, the more difficult it was to follow through on the idea. "The last thing I want to see or feel up close and personal is Alexis's hate," he muttered.

"I think it's a risk you're just going to have to take, or you're going to regret this for the rest of your life, buddy." Mike leaned forward in his chair and braced his arms on the table. "Why do you think she offered you a settlement? Think about it, Jackson. If she knows that the women in your life have always wanted something from you, don't you think this gesture says a whole lot about the kind of woman she is?"

Jackson knew exactly what kind of woman she was. She was caring, open and genuine, and completely opposite to the kind of women who'd been a part of his past. She'd listened, she'd cared and she'd fallen in love with *him*. Her generosity and professional courtesy now didn't surprise him because that was the kind of person she was, and it hit him like a sucker punch to the stomach to realize that she hadn't taken anything from him, but had given more than she'd received. And now, she was offering him enough money that the financial stability of her company would be threatened. The gesture was as selfless as the woman who'd issued it.

I love you. Her words had haunted him since the morning she'd spoken the declaration, pulling on emotions he'd kept deeply buried for so long. He needed her, in ways that might terrify him, but the thought of spending the rest of his life without her, terrified him more.

Mike was right. And so was Merrilee. He did owe Alexis, more than a few words of apology scribbled on a note card attached to a bouquet of flowers. He owed her honesty and the truth. And ultimately, his trust. *In person.* Rejecting him wouldn't be an option he'd let her consider.

"How about another beer?" Mike asked, lifting his empty bottle. "This one's on me."

"I think I'll pass." Jackson stood, more than willing to risk everything for the woman who'd stolen his heart. "There's a fantasy or two between Alexis and me that I still need to tend to."

Mike grinned like a fool. "It's about damn time you came to your senses."

ALEX SAT in her office at Gametek, staring at the phone number Merrilee had given her when Alex had called her a few days ago. Three days, to be exact, and she couldn't put off the inevitable much longer. She'd made a personal vow to tell Jackson the truth if she was pregnant, and her doctor had confirmed her condition with a blood test. She was, undoubtedly, going to have a baby.

The occasion had been marked with unadulterated joy because she finally had something of her own to love and give her that sense of family she'd lived so many years without. But the realization that she was going to have Jackson's baby was underscored with a wealth of insecurities. There was every chance that Jackson might not be interested in being a part of his child's life, and while she couldn't imagine him spurning his own flesh and blood, the possibility did exist. As did the possibility of a custody suit if he decided he wanted his baby, and not her. Yet despite her valid fears, he had every right to know he was going to be a father, and like everything else in her life, she'd deal with the consequences as they arose.

Her throat grew tight, her heart heavy, her eyes a little bit weepy—hormones, she told herself as thoughts of Jackson filtered through her mind. She'd received his flowers and apology, and while it had been a nice, polite gesture on his part, it hadn't been enough to convince her that he wanted her in the same way she ached for him. She wanted, *needed*, his love and trust, and there had been absolutely nothing in his short, curt message to indicate he was willing to give her any of her deepest heart's desires.

She fiddled with the paper with Jackson's phone number on it as her mind drifted back to yesterday's lunch with Dennis and how her VP had nearly choked on his sandwich when she'd told him she was pregnant. They'd always been honest with each other, and her condition certainly wasn't something she could keep a secret forever. For the first time since arriving home from Florida, she'd divulged the details of her fantasy vacation to Dennis, and her involvement with Jackson. To say that Dennis had been shocked was an understatement. He'd been speechless. But once he'd recovered, his protective instincts had kicked in and he'd been coddling her ever since—which was equally trying on her fragile nerves. Alex knew it was only a matter of time before Dennis asked her to marry him, and she'd have to turn him down because there was only one man she loved and she wouldn't marry another out of convenience.

Dennis also didn't understand why she was offering Jackson such a huge out-of-court settlement, but his confusion didn't concern Alex because the only one who needed to understand the sacrifice was Jackson himself. But considering she hadn't heard from him since her attorneys had made the offer to Extreme Software, she suspected he wasn't impressed with her overture or the meaning behind it.

Yawning, she slumped forward in her chair, folded her hands on the top of her desk, and rested her weary head on her arms. It was only eleven in the morning, but all she wanted to do these days was take naps and rest her tired, pregnant body. The past three weeks had not only been physically exhausting, but also emotionally draining, and as a result she felt like an absolute slug. Her lashes drifted shut. Just a few minutes rest, then she'd call Jackson and tell him about their baby....

Sometime later, the sound of loud voices drifting from the reception area woke her from sleep with a start. She straightened slowly, easing the kinks from her body and trying to clear her foggy mind. The male voices grew louder...Dennis and someone else who sounded very demanding and insistent. Concerned, she pushed her chair back and stood, intending to investigate the problem. She'd made it halfway across the room when the door burst open, and in walked Jackson holding a black canvas bag with Dennis hot on his heels.

Stunned, Alex came to an abrupt stop and shook her head, certain she was still asleep and her sensual dreams had conjured this gorgeous, sexy man she'd missed so much. That solid build, his sensually cut lips, those dark, striking eyes that she hoped their son or daughter would inherit. Yes, what a lovely dream.

Their gazes met and locked for a timeless moment. The racing of her pulse and the warm, masculine scent of him she remembered so well assured her she was wide awake and he was real.

"You can't just barge in here and do as you please, Mr. Witt," Dennis said heatedly, shattering the breathless moment between the two of them. Obviously, Jackson had introduced himself to her VP, and

Dennis wasn't the least bit happy to meet the man she'd spent a glorious week with.

Jackson turned back to the other man with calm precision. "I just did. And if you don't mind, I'd like to talk to Alexis *privately*." With a light push against Dennis's puffed out chest that sent the other man stumbling back two steps into the hallway, Jackson shut the door and secured the lock.

He looked back at her, his eyes dark and intense, and a fluttering sensation stirred in Alex's belly, making her very aware that they were alone together. She snapped out of her shock when he stepped toward her. Uncertain, she stepped back. Then she jumped when Dennis pounded his fist against the door.

"I demand that you open this door immediately, or I'm calling the police." The door shook and Alex cringed as he pummeled it once more. "Alex, are you okay in there?"

She wasn't at all threatened by Jackson's presence, but what was left of her aching heart was at risk of breaking completely. "I'm fine, Dennis," she called, loud enough for him to hear. "I'll let you know if there's a problem."

She heard her VP grumble something, then everything went blessedly quiet out in the hallway.

"He really is fond of you." An amused smile quirked the corner of Jackson's mouth. "And I can hardly blame him for wanting to protect you from me."

The husky timbre of his voice caused a delicious shiver to ripple through her. "What he doesn't understand is that I'm more than capable of taking care of myself."

"That's one thing I've come to admire about you."

She frowned, feeling off-balance, by his unannounced visit and how casual and amicable he was being—as if he hadn't left her hanging for the three longest weeks of her life, only to reappear as if dropping by her office was a daily occurrence. Why he was here was the big question. Needing physical distance, she turned and crossed the room to the relative safety behind her desk, feeling his heated gaze on her every step of the way.

"You're back to wearing your loose, flowing skirts," he commented lightly.

She faced him again and shrugged. "They're comfortable." Especially against her stomach. While she hadn't gained any weight yet as a result of her pregnancy, there was no one she wanted to impress here at the office so she opted for practical over fashionable. Those outfits she'd worn at Seductive Fantasy for Jackson were tucked away in her closet, memories of another time, another place...and of a man who'd inspired her more sensual side.

His gaze touched on her hair, then traveled over her face and lingered on her lips. "But you're still wearing your hair down. I like it that way."

Her mouth thinned with barely suppressed irritation. "I find it hard to believe you traveled thousands of miles to critique my appearance."

He sighed and set his black bag on her desk, then strolled to the window overlooking the city. "No, I didn't. I'm here on business."

Her stomach lurched and prickles of dread skittered across her skin. She sat down in her chair, preparing herself for the worst. A part of her had hoped he was here for personal reasons, but it was apparent the whole tangled mess between Gametek and Extreme Software was far from over, despite Fred Hobson being prosecuted for his part in the piracy.

She swallowed to ease the dryness in her mouth. "Did you receive my settlement offer?"

He pushed his hands into the pockets of his slacks and inclined his head. "I did."

She waited for him to explain, but as the seconds ticked by she grew impatient. "Then why are you here?" She didn't mean to sound annoyed, but her nerves were nearly frayed having him so near and not being able to touch him, kiss him, and reaffirm how much she loved him.

"To make you a counteroffer," he said.

She sucked in a quick breath. The pain that sliced through her was excruciating. He wasn't there for *her*; he wanted more than what she'd proposed, obviously needing something more substantial to compensate for something being taken from him, despite her indirect involvement. *Oh, God.* Gametek was on the verge of bankruptcy because of her original offer, her company's financial stability on shaky ground. Anything more would wipe her out completely.

With her insides quaking, how she remained calm and composed was beyond her. "Couldn't our respective attorneys have handled your counter request?"

"I suppose they could have, but I had an appointment to meet with a realtor for a vacation home in La Jolla, and I'm thinking about getting a twenty-six foot cruiser, too. I hear it's warm in San Diego even in the wintertime, which would be a pleasant change from winters in Atlanta.''

He had to be joking about a vacation home and boat near San Diego, near where she *lived*, yet his expression was dead serious. And why was he telling her any of this anyway? To torment her further?

She folded her hands on top of her desk, clenching her fingers tight. "What is your counteroffer, Jackson?"

He rubbed a finger along his jaw, his eyes latching onto hers. "I want to buy out Gametek."

Her mouth literally dropped open, but no words emerged. She could only stare at Jackson, her head spinning with disbelief. Then reality settled in, and so did fury. She wouldn't give up the company she'd worked so hard to make her own. Not without a fight. *"No."*

"Why not?" he asked, his tone reasonable as he circled around to stand in front of her desk again. "Your gaming software is off the market because it lacks my technology, and my technology is a perfect fit for your gaming software. *Zantoid* was on the verge of tremendous success, and I can't think of a better way to make sure we both reap the benefits of our hard work."

He was going to take away her business and strip her of every last shred of dignity. And she wouldn't allow it. The emotions of the past few weeks simmered within her, demanding release. Standing abruptly, she rounded her desk until she was standing inches away and he could feel the full brunt of her anger.

"Damn you, Jackson!" She jabbed a finger against his chest, gratified to see him wince. "How dare you come here thinking that you can take advantage of me and this situation!"

He caught her wrist before her finger drilled a hole through his chest. "I thought it was a great idea," he said gently.

She searched his expression, wondering if the tenderness she detected in his eyes was a figment of her imagination.

His thumb stroked across the rapid pulse in her wrist, and his voice softened, as did his incredible blue eyes. "Maybe I forgot to mention that I'd like you to be a part of the package deal, too?"

The fight drained out of her, but the confusion remained. "You...you want me to *work* for you?"

An adorable smile appeared. "Work for me, marry me...same thing."

Marry him. Her world tipped on its axis, and while elation blossomed within her, her emotions were still tempered by the need to know that there was something far more substantial behind his proposal than a merging of companies.

When she didn't verbally respond, he tipped his head, his expression wry. "I guess I have some explaining to do, huh?"

She nodded jerkily, refusing to make any of this easy on him. Refusing, too, to leap into his arms, as he clearly expected, until she had everything she wanted from him in return.

Reluctantly, he released her hand, but they remained connected by their gazes. "I'm not a fantasy man, Alexis. I'm flesh and blood real, and being human I made a huge mistake by judging you before I even knew you, based on past experiences. And I hate that I hurt you. I'm so very sorry for that. Can you ever forgive me?"

"I already have," she whispered.

"I'm truly a lucky man." He brushed his knuckles down her cheek in a reverent caress. "All my life I've felt as though I've been used for one thing or another, but now I want to give and share, and do so freely. With you. Just so long as you'll accept the real me in return."

The hint of vulnerability she detected endeared him to her all the more. "I want the *real* Jackson, not some fantasy man. And there's only one thing I'll ever want from you."

His thumb feathered across her bottom lip, kindling a warmth and desire that surged through her veins. "And what's that?" he murmured.

"Your love."

"That's a given. It took me way too long to admit my feelings, to myself and to you, but I do love you." He picked up her hand and pressed her palm against his chest, right over his rapidly beating heart. "I love you, Alexis Baylor, with my heart, my soul, with everything that I am." His declaration shone in his eyes, leaving no doubts between them.

"Then how about your trust?"

He moved closer, backing her up against the edge of her desk, his hard thighs aligning with hers. "I wouldn't be here if I didn't trust and believe in you."

A hot, sexual frisson of excitement and awareness shot through her, and she struggled to keep her mind on important matters. "I know that, but I wanted to make sure you knew it, too."

"Oh, I do," he assured her.

Grasping her waist, he lifted her up and scooted her bottom back so she was sitting on the surface of her desk. She gasped in surprise, and he merely grinned, a sexy, lazy smile full of confidence and just a bit of sin. He lowered his head and kissed her lightly on the lips, much too lightly to appease Alex's restless need.

"I'm hoping I can do something that will ultimately prove my love," he said between soft kisses, "and just how much I trust and believe in us together, for a lifetime."

She closed her eyes and parted her lips, which he traced lazily with his tongue. "Merge our companies?"

He dragged the material of her skirt up, just enough that he could nudge his way between her smooth thighs until they were pressed intimately together. "Merge *us.*"

Her lashes fluttered open as joy filled her entire being. She tightened her legs around his flanks and looped her arms around his neck to keep him close. "Oh, I like the sound of that," she said in a sexy purr of sound, her body craving the heat and strength of his.

She pulled him down for a welcome home kiss, and they both got lost in the wondrous pleasure of being together again. Breathless minutes later, he pulled back, and she protested with a soft whimper of sound.

He pressed his forehead against hers, trying to rein in his slip of control. "You're distracting me from my original purpose."

She slid her lips along his jaw, then nipped on his earlobe as her hands stroked over his firm buttocks. "You were talking about merging *us*," she reminded him.

"Oh, yeah." He groaned when she rubbed her softness deliberately against him, making him impossibly harder. "Alexis...first things first." He stilled her movements and looked deeply into her eyes. "'I love you' merged our hearts, and I want to give you something that will merge our souls."

"Then we merge our bodies?" she asked impatiently.

His laugh was strained as he unzipped the bag on her desk and dug through the contents. "Oh, yeah. That'll be the best part. But humor me, and let me do this in the right order." Finding what he needed, he handed her a flat, square gold-foil box the size of her hand, tied off with a shimmery gold ribbon.

She looked from the gift, to him, delight and confusion mingling across her features. "What's this? Another surprise?"

"The best one of them all." He tucked a wisp of hair behind her ear, just as an excuse to touch her. "It's proof of my love and my commitment to you."

When she merely stared at the box, he gave it a nudge. "Open it, sweetheart."

The ribbon unraveled with a quick tug. Like an excited child on Christmas morning, she lifted the lid and peered inside. She gasped, her eyes wide as she glanced from the contents, to him, and back again. Nestled in the middle of the box of chocolates was a two-carat diamond ring.

"Oh, Jackson," she breathed, her eyes brimming with tears as the significance of his gift registered. "Amaretto truffles." She swallowed, but that didn't stop the trickle of a tear from slipping down her cheek.

He wiped away the moisture with his thumb. "And an engagement ring," he said, making sure she knew exactly what kind of ring he was offering her. He plucked the bridal set from the box and grasped her trembling left hand in his. "Marry me, Alexis. I promise to keep this box of truffles filled and never let it go empty for as long as you'll have me."

She bit her bottom lip and nodded jerkily. "Yes, I'll marry you."

An inexplicable feeling expanded Jackson's chest as he slipped the sparkling ring on her finger and claimed this incredible woman as his own. "You're supposed to be happy, not crying."

"I *am* happy," she assured him with a sniffle. "And I'm sure all this excess crying is hormonal, just a symptom of pregnancy."

It took an extra heartbeat for her words to sink in. "You're pregnant?"

She nodded, looking slightly worried. "It was

originally part of my fantasy," she admitted. "I wanted a baby, something to call my own. I wanted that closeness of family...Jackson, getting pregnant was the farthest thing from my mind when we made love, but I'm not sorry I'm carrying your child. Not when I love you so much."

An elated shudder passed through his body, and he cupped her face between his palms, making sure she looked directly at him. "A family," he said, his tone awed. "Alexis, you've given me the greatest gift of all, and more than I ever dreamed I'd have."

She pressed a hand to her midsection and smiled, brightening his life. "I'll give you as many of these gifts as you'd like. Personally, I'd be happy with half a dozen."

"Oh, yeah." Still astonished that he'd created such a miracle, he dropped his hands and gently slipped them under her untucked blouse. He glided his warm palms over her ribs, then down, dragging the waistband of her skirt over her hips, and lower, until he could touch her belly without any barriers and cradle the life growing within.

A lump formed in his throat as he withdrew his probing fingers and glanced back up at Alexis. "How have I lived my entire life without you in it?"

"I think we were waiting for each other," she said, and he knew it was true. "The past is the past, Jackson, and now neither one of us has to spend another day alone. You've merged our hearts, our souls, our companies...there's just one more thing to merge to complete the deal."

The sassy look in her eyes tempted and teased

him. He grinned, ready and willing to accommodate her—now and for the rest of their lives together.

"Yes, ma'am." Sweeping her off the desk and into his arms, he carried her over to the executive sofa at the far end of the room where he spent the next hour sealing a lifetime deal.

* * * * *

The Fantasy continues:

SECRET FANTASY

By Carly Phillips
Available June 2001

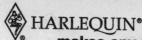

Harlequin truly does
make any time special. . . .
This year we are celebrating
weddings in style!

To help us celebrate, we want you to tell us how wearing the Harlequin wedding gown will make your wedding day special. As the grand prize, Harlequin will offer one lucky bride the chance to **"Walk Down the Aisle"** in the Harlequin wedding gown!

There's more...

For her honeymoon, she and her groom will spend five nights at the **Hyatt Regency Maui.** As part of this five-night honeymoon at the hotel renowned for its romantic attractions, the couple will enjoy a candlelit dinner for two in Swan Court, a sunset sail on the hotel's catamaran, and duet spa treatments.

Maui • Molokai • Lanai

To enter, please write, in, 250 words or less, how wearing the Harlequin wedding gown will make your wedding day special. The entry will be judged based on its emotionally compelling nature, its originality and creativity, and its sincerity. This contest is open to Canadian and U.S. residents only and to those who are 18 years of age and older. There is no purchase necessary to enter. Void where prohibited. See further contest rules attached. Please send your entry to:

Walk Down the Aisle Contest

In Canada
P.O. Box 637
Fort Erie, Ontario
L2A 5X3

In U.S.A.
P.O. Box 9076
3010 Walden Ave.
Buffalo, NY 14269-9076

You can also enter by visiting www.eHarlequin.com
Win the Harlequin wedding gown and the vacation of a lifetime!
The deadline for entries is October 1, 2001.

HARLEQUIN®
Makes any time special ®

PHWDACONT1